Win Win

A True Story by

William Gage

intro

You are about to be taken on a journey and if you approach it with your heart and mind open then you will receive priceless knowledge. From there you can use that gift to change your life.

This book may start a bit slow for some but it soon warms up and will take you to amazing destinations. The world is a rapidly changing place and as governments constantly seize your legal and human rights and put you under increasingly invasive surveillance it is very much in your interests to add to your knowledge in equal measures. I am not a psychic or a genius but I do have many lessons for you.

Ever since I was a young boy I've been analysing and asking deep questions. Like most people do, I wonder why we are all here on this Earth. I wonder what we are meant to do, what we are meant to learn, how we are supposed to learn it and where we go next whether we manage to learn or not.

I wonder whether fate acts upon people in order to allow each individual to experience, to learn and thus to teach others. The others in turn can gain from the knowledge without having to live the experience whether it was positive or negative.

I personally believe that we are all here to live, to learn and to teach. Today is my birthday I'm 37 years old. That is a relatively young age yet I have had some extreme experiences both positive and negative. Perhaps it was my fate that brought me those experiences and I may have a duty to pass on the lessons learned. The great thing is that I don't have to speak to just one person these pages allow me to touch an infinite number of you.

In order to show you the full picture I must go back to the early 1990's and describe some significant events in my life. I will try to keep them as brief as possible to bring you up to speed and show you my first experience of the justice system where my eyes were opened. And if you seek then the first lessons are there to be discovered.

I hope that you will keep an open mind and that you will persevere at the beginning and journey through enjoy the story and hopefully receive your message. Whoever you may be dear pupil I dedicate this work to you. Fate will no doubt put this story in your hands and will let you wake up and learn the lesson that is meant just for you. Take it, use it, I send it with love.

If someone else had written this book and I read it in my early teens then I would have lived my life in an entirely different way avoiding mountains of pain. I hope that many others manage to find and read it and I pray that growth and a thirst for knowledge are sparked within them. As the saying goes, a wise man will learn from his mistakes, a shrewd man will also learn from the mistakes of others.

William Gage 1st March 2008

1 Hands of Fate

In 1994 I was 23 years old. For the past five years I had been partying I was in pubs and nightclubs at least three nights per week sometimes more. Drugs never did it for me and neither did hard spirits, I prefer to stay aware so I just drank beer.

There was a recession on at that time and most workers were feeling the pinch. I was doing alright, I had bundles of good quality clothes and had worked my way up to owning a 7 series BMW. Back then it was a tool of a car for a young man.

Glasgow can be a violent city and when you spend so much time out on the town partying you inevitably end up involved. Despite the statistics it is an acknowledged fact by everyone who knows me that I have never wilfully started a fight in my life. There have been a couple of occasions when I have asked enemies if they fancy a dash however if they decline then I walk away.

I only ever attack people who are either attacking me or attacking my friends. It is for that very reason that I rarely ever lose. I last lost a fight in 1983 when a few older boys kicked me all over Great Western road. Since that night I have always avoided causing trouble and have so far came out on top after every battle. I do regret the fact that I ever had to do damage but I admit freely that once it kicks off I like to win. I never start it, I always try to avoid it but once it's on I don't mind telling you that I hate trouble makers and bullies and I used to beat up such characters.

My life has brought me some amazing experiences from absolute mayhem in the middle of running battles to good wages and the freedom that they provide, to beautiful women far travels and good friends to the adrenalin thunderstorm that comes with armed robbery to life on top then down to the bottom in dark dungeons then back up with a period of learning and an intellectual and spiritual awakening to a new life full of positive pursuits and love.

I do not tolerate injustice and in my younger years I would burst bullies and leave them on the pavement. As I learned more and opened up my mind I recognised the ugliness of violence and I found that my true sword was the pen.

Inevitably I focused on tyrants.

Being bullies and troublemakers themselves the establishment see people like me as a threat and that is the reason why I have so many kindred spirits in jail doing agonisingly long sentences while at the same time monsters who prey upon the vulnerable are consistently given a slap on the wrist with lenient sentences. I will expand on all of that later and allow you the chance to come to your own conclusions.

In 1994 fate chose to teach me some harsh lessons. One night I was in a club with three friends, we only wanted to score with some birds have a couple of beers then get kebabs on the way home. Unfortunately someone was up to no good inside the club and he got a punch on the nose. The bouncers came over and politely asked us to leave so we did. I have found many bouncers to be bullies and woman beaters so I used to like to fight them more than any other sort of adversaries. This mob were polite enough and only doing their job so we were obligingly allowing them to escort us out of the door.

One of them turned out to be a bad robot. The last one of us who was leaving the club is only five eight tall and no more than about nine stone. The bad bouncer could not resist his bully instincts he grabbed my friend then tried to close the doors with him trapped inside. No doubt the intent was to give the wee man a kicking. I managed to grab my pal's arm and we had a tug of war. My two other friends managed to hold the doors open long enough for me to pull him free. The bouncer made the mistake of stepping one foot out past the doorway. He was sprayed with pepper spray and given a punch to the top of the head which knocked him back. The punch was helped by a diamond ring which split a wound in his head. The wound immediately sent blood rolling down his face. The other bouncers pulled him back and managed to slam the doors shut.

As we walked away we could hear screaming coming from up on the main road. Two birds were standing over a guy who was laying in the middle of the road, he had been stabbed in some other fight. Typical Glasgow. The police and ambulance had already been called to the stabbing even before we had started with the bouncers. The four of us were not able to help them and piled into my friend's car which was a two door.

I got in the back and as I looked out of the back window I could see the police cars arriving at the stabbing. I then saw the bouncer covered in blood running over to the police.

We got trapped at the very next red light and the police cars quickly appeared and surrounded our car. The victim of the stabbing was abandoned and the bouncer had been given a lift by the police. They obviously saw the blood-covered bouncer as one of their own and viewed him not only as a priority but they had also let him come along for some badness. Within seconds there were about eight police standing round our car. One of them yanked the passenger door open and two others grabbed one of my friends by the arms and dragged him half of the way out of the car where they held him firm with his arms spread out wide. The bouncer had a long metal torch and he absolutely destroyed my friend's face with five big full power hammer blows. The force smashed his nose all over his face and sprayed blood everywhere. One of the police eventually shouted, "That's good enough!" and pulled the bouncer away.

The rest of us were dragged out of the car. My friend was now covered in blood and his face was smashed to bits. His nose is spread out flat over his face to this day. Even though he was leathered he stood tall, spat out a mouthful of blood and said to the bouncer, "That was really stupid." The bouncer lunged for me and I managed to get one hand free from the police grip. He swung the torch at my face and I raised my hand up in defence. The blow caused an agonising crack in my hand. The police were satisfied and pulled him back again.

They cuffed me and pushed me towards a police van that had arrived. I turned round to the bouncer and smiled, "You've made a mistake idiot." He could see that we could take the beating and the arrest and that we were not affected too much and were in fact promising him a further dash. His face began to lose it's mask of aggression and he started to sober up as he realised that this was not over and that we would take revenge. We were all taken to Stewart Street police station where I couldn't resist arguing with them about why they had ignored the poor guy who lay stabbed in the street and why they were more interested in helping a bully boy bouncer. I told them that I believed that it all said a great deal about their own shitty characters and the evil stares began to meet my every gaze. They were not happy with me at all. I was not yet fully aware of just how upset they were. They put me in a cell where I quickly forgot the provocation that I had dished up and I stupidly drifted into a beer assisted sleep. The boots to the face woke me up. One fat copper was standing right on top of me making it almost impossible to breathe while his colleagues took penalty kicks into me from every angle. It was not a fight therefore not a loss. It was over quickly but now I was splattered with my own blood. I stayed awake after that and some hours later the throbbing in my hand from the battering with the torch began to get too much to take and I showed it to the turnkey. God knows how my friend managed to handle that same pain all over his face and specifically his nose. Eye-watering agony. It must be the West Ham thug in him.

I was taken to the Royal Infirmary where they told me that I had broken one of the long bones between my knuckle and wrist. They assured me that it would heal itself and sent me on my way with my two bored police escorts. I caught a glimpse of a mirror on the way out and noticed the tell tale black lines all over my face. When the police polish their boots some of that polish is soaked up by the rubber at the edge of the sole. When they boot into you the polish is brought out of the sole as it comes into contact with the hard surface of your face and head. That is what causes the black lines that you see on the faces of many prisoners outside the back doors of police stations who are getting on the bus to go to court. I looked a right state. This was not turning out to be a very good night on the town.

Due to the fact that we had taken it tight and that the police had actually driven the bouncer in their own police car to attack us, we were all granted bail. The Crown later dropped the charges against my friend who had suffered the smashed nose and face. They wanted to keep that part of the story hidden.

Some weeks later I was in another nightclub during a weeknight. I was with just one friend and he is not one who likes to fight. I looked over and there was some of the bouncers from the other club on a work night out unfortunately the bad bouncer who had started it all was not there with them. I told my friend to sit back and not get involved but give him his due he refused and insisted that he would help me. I walked over and reminded them who I was then asked them if they fancied a dash. None of them had been involved in the fight that is why I was asking politely rather than just get right into round two. They didn't fancy it so I left it out. I did ask them to get on the phone to their tough guy pal and tell him to come up here to see me. I left them to it and enjoyed the rest of the night. Fifteen minutes before closing time I walked back over and told them that I would be leaving in fifteen so I wanted them to phone their pal and get him ready for me coming out. I was still really angry about what he had done and wanted another go with him.

I never phoned anyone for help. I have never called for help in my life. My philosophy has always been that you need to chuck it if you cant at least make the effort to meet anything and anyone head on even when you are alone unarmed and at your weakest. If you are in that state and end up in front of an armed foe or a large amount of enemies then you should try to escape however you should at least have the courage to stand up and have a go at it. You can only be destroyed once. I stepped out alone and walked straight into thin air! He couldn't find the balls to turn up even when he had me on a plate. Not so tough without his police friends and his bouncer title to protect him from the courts.

The hands of fate were not so shy. They touched me again two months later. I drove two of my friends into town in my car and we met up with another one who parked his car in front of mine. We went to a nightclub that we had never visited before. It was a favourite of football players and plastic people. The birds were mostly gold diggers and we were not impressed. I had a nice BMW outside, I happened to be carrying a few quid on me and I was doing well. Thankfully the birds couldn't see the car or the money they could only see my jeans and t-shirt. One good looking bird caught my eye but she walked straight past and stood eyeing up a guy in a white suit. He looked to me like a giro punter who sells a bit of gear and pretends to be Tony Montana. She was clearly digging for gold so he was welcome to her.   That summed the club right up really. It was mostly full of these characters who may have earned good pay but they showed no style and appeared to have no character underneath the labels. That made them skint in my eyes.

We left early and drove along the road to a kebab shop. We parked at either side of the road. After eating our food two friends got inside my car. I said goodbye to the other one and no sooner had I turned away when I heard a distinctive rumble. I spun back round to see a big skinhead bashing a sealed can of cola into my friends head while gripping him tight by the scruff of the neck. I joined in and managed to take the can from him and throw it away across the road. The two others jumped out of my car and two friends of the skinhead also rushed over. We had a good fight that took us from the front of the kebab shop across the road and then up into the entrance of a wide lane. The skinhead pulled out a small knife. As soon as my friend caught sight of the silver blade he snatched it from the mug cutting his own hand in the process. They struggled on and he stabbed the skinhead once with his own knife. They struggled further and I managed to get between them and took the knife from my friend and tossed it away up into the darkness of the lane before he could do any more unnecessary damage.

Stabbing is a shit-bag move. It makes no sense and in an instant it can turn a good fight into an unnecessary death and a life sentence. The victim doesn't even feel the wound so it's not even an effective fighting technique. When people are slashed it has an immediate shock affect on their nervous system and that often causes them to lose the fight, they are left with a scar to remind them to behave themselves in future, I am not condoning slashing as a fight technique I can understand it. Stabbing is completely different, it is a pointless cowardly move unless you really want to kill the other guy. Stop stabbing people young team it is a shit-bag's way to fight. Use your head and your courage. There is no need to act like cowards. Stop stabbing people.

The fight lasted for another minute or so when one of us (who has a really bad temper) knocked one of them out then ran over and cracked the skinhead square on the chin and knocked him out, it was surreal. I was still raging about what he had done with that can of cola so I broke the rules and gave him a full force penalty kick to the side while he lay there helpless. I was trying to give him a painful set of ribs which would hopefully last a few days. His bird was not happy about that kick and she ran towards me shouting about killing me. She had long red hair (psycho Scotswoman) and was screaming. I detest men who harm women and I had no wish to do such an unnatural thing so I ran away and she chased me round a parked car, to the delight of the crowd of spectators who were now laughing uncontrollably at me running away like a big poof.

She was right and I was wrong, I should never have taken such a liberty kicking the guy when he was down and unconscious. Truth be told I had been shocked by the initial attack which had come from nowhere and fear turns to evil rather quickly hence the kick to the helpless victim. We left the skinhead and his friends on the pavement and jumped into our cars and drove away. Later that night the police seized my car off the street. Someone in the kebab shop had noted my registration number.

The police caught up with me a few months later and by that time my court date had come up for the other fight with the bouncers. The trial for the bouncers fight was to be held in the dreaded Glasgow Sheriff Court, a stinking freezing horrible cathedral of injustice.

As already stated the charges had been dropped against the boy with the smashed nose and face in order to keep that part of the story hidden from the jury. That left me and the other two in the dock. After only one day the charges were dropped against them and the Crown gunned for me on my own. The other bouncers were decent enough and never went out of their way to help the Crown. The bad one went all of the way and told lies for the police as he exaggerated and even cried while he gave evidence! A completely different figure from the torch wielding, face smashing animal who we had seen. He had a small star shaped scar underneath his hair where I had punched him. The surgeon who had treated that wound said that it was absolutely the result of blunt force trauma which could have come from a heavy fall against a hard surface or from a heavy blow like a punch. The police produced two lock back knifes and told the jury that they both had traces of the victim's blood on the blade. He only had one blunt force trauma wound and none of us had any of his blood on our skin or clothes. He had not even been hit with a knife and we had no knifes on us. There were no fingerprints or fibres on either of the two knifes, surprise - surprise.

Even when you are guilty and they have you bang to rights the police and prosecutors often cant help themselves. They are steeped so deeply in a culture of lies and deceit that they have to manufacture ridiculous false evidence in an effort to make things worse for the accused.   If you happen to know anyone who has been a defendant in Scotland then ask them what sort of skulduggery their police and prosecutors were up to and you will see just how prevalent these corrupt practices really are.

Prosecutors always exaggerate the charges and this one was accusing me of serious assault and permanent disfigurement. The Sheriff asked the bouncer to show him this disfigurement and the bouncer made a feeble attempt to hold back his hair in order to show the court his scar. The surgeon had told the court that the scar was star shaped but no one could see the silly wee thing.

The Sheriff ordered the prosecutor to delete the words permanent disfigurement from the indictment.   That left me facing the charge of serious assault. One punch to this bully's head was one hundred times less serious assault than being held firm by the police and have your face smashed to bits by this very man who was now standing here crying and pretending to be a poor victim.

Make your own enquiries and come to your own conclusions. In my experience such disgusting lies and deceit are the norm. Such is the state of our justice system and it's culture of lies exaggeration and absolute injustice. Don't just take my word on that. Investigate.

The prosecutor had also listed three charges under the firearms act. My lawyer said that since the pepper spray sent out a projectile (the liquid pepper) then it was in fact a firearm according to the law. I had no way of knowing if such a ridiculous law existed or if this was simply another case of a prosecutor telling lies and trying to make everything look worse. A police weapons expert gave evidence and made the pepper spray sound so lethal that it was just one step less serious than a flame-thrower. The surgeon who had treated the bouncer said that his eyes were not stinging or watering when he arrived at hospital only ten minutes after the fight.

A real lethal weapon. Weeks later the police themselves were all issued with pepper spray and strangely enough they had another expert. This one spoke to the media and said that the spray was simply a self defence tool for momentarily incapacitating your attacker.

After all of the police lies and the help from the crying bouncer the jury believed the Crown and came back with a guilty verdict. I would have pled guilty to what I had genuinely done and it would be a shorter sentence. Their bogus and exaggerated charges and their culture of lies prevented me from helping them with any guilty plea. I was given nine months imprisonment for one punch and six months on each of the three firearms act charges all to run concurrent. Some people have looked at a list of my previous convictions and seeing the three firearms act charges and not realising that it was just a daft pepper spray they presume that I have had some involvement or some fascination with guns. Please get your facts right before you speak lest you inadvertently spread police propaganda and do me unnecessary harm.

For one punch onto the head of a bully boy bouncer they sent me to Hell. Her Majesty's prison Barlinnie in Glasgow has seen more anguish terror and torture than any other part of Scotland. It was an absolute hellhole where the real world is far away in an impossible to reach Galaxy.

I was placed into 'A' hall in December 1994. Barlinnie holds roughly 1000 prisoners who are either on remand not yet having been tried, or who are convicted already having been sentenced to less than four years. Many ex-cons refer to certain prisons as hate factories and no one could disagree with that description of Barlinnie. The convicted prisoners are all forced to wear red shirts. The big cell doors and all of the railings were also painted red. Any psychologist will tell you that the colour red makes people angry.

Back then the cells had not been painted for at least the past 20 years and the walls were covered in thick grime. The entire place was teeming with rats; cats pigeons cockroaches maggots and flies. Worst of all though was the majority of the screws. They exercised a brutal reign of absolute terror. Try to find anyone who was in there at that time for a more detailed description of this hell on earth. The screws were monsters and they would lock up each hall several times per day and would storm into one cell mob handed to batter brutalise and torture unfortunate individuals at random. Some prisoners were even raped.

The prison Doctor eventually resigned and went public with his statement of reasons. He told the media that he was treating battered and tortured prisoners who had serious injuries every day of the week and most of the injuries had admittedly been inflicted by the warders. No one really listened, no one cared. The media only gave the story a couple of lines. It was just criminals who were being tortured after all they seemed to be hinting.

Yet more than fifty percent of the prisoners inside Barlinnie were doing less than six months for minor offences like road traffic crime and non payment of fines for vandalism or minor acts of theft or fraud. In other words the majority of the prisoners were otherwise ordinary members of the public who just happened to be down on their luck and who have happened to fall foul of the law at a minor level.

The fact that the public did not seem to care made me realise just how successful the establishment had been in getting the media to terrorise the public with so many scare stories about so many dangerous criminals that some people had now lost touch with reality and humanity and were actually happy to see a prison regime that pretended to be 'tough on crime and tough on criminals' when in actual fact it was a torture factory.

During my first year in Barlinnie the brutality and the terror caused seven human beings to give up and destroy themselves by committing suicide. The majority of the remainder were psychologically damaged to some degree. Many were damaged to a large degree and the weird thing is that many of the very people who had been happy to hear of prisoners being physically battered and tortured in such a 'tough' prison regime found out that no one should ever commit torture. Most of the victims of it would explode their bottled up rage as soon as they were set free and would pass the wickedness onto the next victim in line. Think about it rationally, how can such an evil place do any good for the average person or for society in general? It cant.

So the tough regime which is allegedly intended to protect the public literally warps the minds of it's victims and causes a great many of them to victimise others in the future. I will explain later why I believe that our rulers have been actively using such an apparently backwards and detrimental system in the full knowledge of the harm that it causes.

In Barlinnie I took heed of wise words that I had heard years ago. My teacher had suffered the injustice of a sentence in the notorious Dover borstal during the early 1980's the time of the 'short sharp shock' treatment made infamous by the film 'Scum'. Screws back there had murdered more than a few young lads by hangings and even by kicking some to death. My teacher survived it and gave me this wise lesson. "If you are ever sent to jail for any reason then be the grey man, blend in and plod along never bite try not to fight and never ever hit any screw. If they do you a really bad turn then be patient and try to wait until you get out then hunt them down. Try to never hit a screw in jail. They are right on offer for you in the street because the bullies are easy to catch. You already know where they work for starters."

I had to repeat those wise words every day in Barlinnie as I witnessed the brutal activities of the majority of the screws and I would personally bite my tongue for the millionth time as the latest coward was growling at me or treating me like a mug. Thankfully the perverted element within the Barlinnie screw gang never tried to harm me physically. I survived and thanks to never trying to touch me future revenge was avoided.

The prisoners were so tightly wound up with the terror that they lashed out at each other. There were stabbings and slashing and fights every single day often more than once per day.

A large amount of prisoners used cannabis to chill out. Other drugs were available on a very small scale including heroin however that is so addictive that it cant be paid for every day so most of the guys who were heroin addicts outside forced themselves to stay off while in jail.

I personally never touch drugs in jail. It is a war to me and I like to stay wide awake and fully operational. Also I never bother with porn magazines, I switch my mind off to all of that. There are no birds available, I mean that there literally are none because I would never give pleasure to a female screw no matter how nice she may look she still locks doors on people and to me that is unnatural. Such behaviour tells me that they are not deserving of pleasure from me. I don't mean to judge them harshly and I don't dislike them for any reason, I simply feel that locking doors is casual inhumanity and any woman who can do that has a questionable character in my mind.

In America they mix the sex offenders right in with the ordinary prisoners that is why you see all of the jail poof activities. England also has a bit of a problem with that. In Scotland the sex offenders are kept separate for their own protection. There are some gay prisoners of course and no one bothers them only latent homos are homophobic. The majority of prisoners have the added frustration of no sex and many use porn magazines and such for relief. I believe that it is best to switch off and be a monk.

There were no televisions in prison back then and I read books. I love books and I had read a few outside. In the cell the written word became my escape. My teachers. My friends. I read one book on average every two to three days. I would read until my eyes were exhausted and refused to focus. I had been more interested in the birds than the lessons at school and since there were no birds for me here I could now devote all of my attention to books. I tried to teach myself to read with intelligence analysing every single word and sentence and story.

Next I started to write. First it was letters full of funny stories or bits of bullshit for a laugh until eventually I started to write short stories. My writing is not the best but it is good enough for the purpose of communication. I never stopped reading and the exercise that my mind was performing was as good as any workout for the muscles in a gym. I managed to gain some control over the stress and strain of the nightmare life in Barlinnie and I began to grow.

I practised yoga once per week with a fantastic teacher who unwittingly saved lives in Barlinnie with her good practice and teachings. May the forces of goodness and light bless you and yours.

Through more and more reading and yoga and light work in the gym I analysed and studied and practised and learned as much as I could about my own body and my mind. I trained in the cell as well as the gym. Every minute was mine not theirs I would use it all for my advantage and my growth.

The stress was immensely powerful and I fought it all to the best of my ability. I studied my fellow prisoners, listened to their stories, tried to learn from their life lessons. And I tried to pass on some lessons that I had learned. I quickly realised that the screws, in their capacity as the front ranks of the establishment inside jail, loved it when prisoners stabbed or slashed each other up. I pointed this out every time that someone copped it and I constantly advised people to only use violence for self-defence.

I was desperately searching for a higher purpose to all of this jail madness and could find none. The regime, the terror and the brutality absolutely destroyed all goodness and replaced it with murderous hate. I even let my guard down on occasion and had a few bad spells myself filled with anger and hate. Thankfully I am lucky enough to have the strength of character to pull myself out of such weak negativity. It is however a lifelong battle and still takes energy.

I continued my quest to read on and analyse and learn as much as possible in order to understand everything and ultimately to overcome this hell and the entire system that had created the torture machine. I looked beyond the screws, beyond the regime, beyond the police the prosecutors and the judges, beyond the government to the Royals who are sat up at the very top of this festering pile. Once there I had to look back beyond our time and into history. Not the unlikely history that we have all been taught. True history can be seen if you just apply yourself and analyse rationally and eradicate everything that is most unlikely to have happened. When you get rid of the unlikely you are left with the possible and from there you can use your own intelligence and insight in order to discover what is most likely the true story.

In January 1995 I appeared in Glasgow High court for the fight outside the kebab shop with the skinhead. None of my three amigos had been found, one had since died and I refused to name the others of course.

The prosecutor true to form had laid the charges on thick and had made it 'attempted murder to severe injury and danger of life'. The skinhead only had one tiny stab wound. It had not hit any organs or arteries and there was no bruise from the hilt of his knife therefore it was not even a heavy blow.

He received a couple of stitches. Attempted murder to severe injury and danger of life! One wee tiny hole with a couple of stitches, these prosecutors should do evening work at the comedy club.

Since the police could not find my friend they got the skinhead to say that I was the one who had stabbed him. His bird and his two friends refused to repeat that lie because they were not chasing criminal injuries money and so had no incentive to commit perjury as moonlight work for Strathclyde's finest. The police can veto claims.

I had snatched the knife from my friend and had actually prevented the skinhead from suffering any more unnecessary stab wounds yet here he was swearing my life away just to earn a few bob from the police. He starts a fight then when he begins to lose he pulls out a knife then when it gets taken off him and he ends up knocked out and beaten he then grasses me and tells lies in court. Real nice guy. When his bird came in to give her evidence I realised why it had all kicked off in the first place. She was a real beauty, her long red hair looked much better in daylight and the fact that she was no longer chasing after me to kill me made her far more attractive.

My friend who the big skinhead had initially attacked, fancies himself as a bit of a shagger so I could now see that my clown pal had said something to the beautiful red haired bird without noticing her fifteen stone moron boyfriend. I was glad to hear that she had now dumped him. Hopefully she never went back, she was far too good looking to be with such a dafty.

By the end of the trial it had come down to my word against his and since he had the entire crown on his side pretending to believe his version of events the majority of the jury went with the crown and came back with a guilty verdict. The judge sentenced me to three years imprisonment. That was in court number one. That very day in court number two a beast was sentenced for standing behind his girlfriend as she sat helpless in a chair and in an unprovoked attack he stabbed her in the head with a solid lock back knife fracturing her skull and almost killing the poor girl. Now that WAS attempted murder and severe injury and danger of life yet that bastard was only sentenced to two years!

There was a huge difference between the two crimes and yet the judges gave me a sentence that was one year more than his and gave him a sentence that in my opinion was five years too short. I began to study such discrepancies and injustices in our system.

I left Glasgow High court and returned to Barlinnie to start my three year sentence. I was really angry about the injustice. I got three years for a stand up fight with a man yet that very day a beast got only two years for actually attempting to murder a poor defenceless girl in an unprovoked attack. He was kept separate from us in court and was hiding in the protection hall. Lucky for him because I was so angry that day that I would have redressed the balance. Over the years I have advised countless people against attacking the monsters who are sometimes caught outside of their protection halls because they are not worth the extra prison sentence. That day I would have gone against all sensible ideas.

The months started to creep past. The horrific regime and the resulting stress took a toll on me just like it did to every other prisoner. I have never met or heard of anyone who has done some jail time and who has not suffered permanent psychological damage. It is well documented that when you bottle up negative emotions you are storing up trouble both physical and psychological. There was no safe way to release the massive amounts of negativity without getting even more time so you had no choice but to bottle it all up and pray that you would not crack up before you could gain your freedom.

The only escape that some prisoners had was cannabis. Roughly about thirty percent of prisoners were cannabis smokers at that time. It seemed to do them some good and they appeared to be more laid back than the rest of us. I must stress that it was cannabis, not the mind bending skunk that puts teenage kids in psychiatric wards these days. You kids should stop smoking that skunk shit if you want to have a working brain in the future. Don't be scared of the world, face up to it in a sober state. Only cowards need to be drunk every week.

Notices went up all over Barlinnie. New rules. The SPS would start doing mandatory drug tests on prisoner's urine. A refusal to provide a sample would result in extra charges (these were the dark days before Scotland signed up to the

Human Rights Act) any sample which proved to be positive for drugs would also result in more time. Cannabis stays in your system for up to twenty-eight days and opiates stay in your system for up to two days.

The more inquisitive among you readers will wonder why we were provided with that information. All will become clear later when I talk about Afghanistan. I wondered what opiates were and I was soon told – Heroin. The thirty percent of prisoners back then who were using cannabis buckled and the new drug testing forced the majority of them to stop immediately.

There were now about three hundred former cannabis smokers suddenly suffering the stresses and strains of the brutal regime. The inevitable happened. Where previously there had been a couple of hundred heroin addicts who had no money to buy it there was no market so most of them had been forced to kick their habits. Now with the drug tests some of the former cannabis smokers gave in to the stress and decided to get some heroin for relief purely because it only stayed in their system for two days and therefore they had a better chance of avoiding extra jail time. They all fully intended to just take a small amount of heroin maybe once per week during the long weekends and every single one of them vowed not to become anything like the junkies who are hooked.

They had money and thus the market was born. Heroin is a plague and once it had a small customer base it quickly seized control of the majority of the prison population. First all of the former cannabis smokers were hooked. Once there was a ready supply the former heroin addicts themselves could now get access to tiny amounts with their canteen money. Next the majority of the rest of the prisoners looked for a release from the terrible pressure of prison life. They tried heroin and were immediately hooked. It all happened at a staggeringly quick pace and almost without noticing we suddenly had a prison population that was now made up of ninety percent heroin addicts. Straight guys would come in the door doing a few weeks jail on a reckless driving speeding charge, they would buckle under the strain, try heroin and would join the masses who were hooked. After release they would go through the classic meltdown, lose their job, lose their dignity, lose their loved ones then lose themselves into a desperate life of petty crime and heroin abuse. The plague is far more powerful than any mere mortal who ever tries to dance with it.

During the first weeks of the plague I had one cellmate who offered me some heroin. The stress in jail is so extreme that it is sorely tempting to try anything for just one small relief. I was tempted however I suddenly pictured my Dad looking in through the cell window. He is my best friend and is the strongest and kindest man that I have ever met. I then pictured my Mum, her beautiful spirit heals any pain whenever she is near. She is a gentle wee angel just like her own mother was. I love my Mum and Dad dearly and it was with a vision of them in my mind that my life was saved when I managed to refuse the poison that is heroin. I knew that my parents if they could see in the cell window would want to see me fit and strong in a sober state of mind. They would not want to see me trying to escape with the false route of drugs like some weakling maggot. I knew that they would want to see me reading, studying, learning, training in the gym, doing Yoga, thinking positively, being optimistic and feeling love not hate. And I determined to live up to any positive expectations such as those that they may have.

I refused the gear and have never been remotely tempted ever since that night. Unfortunately ninety percent of my fellow prisoners were not so cautious or so lucky. They foolishly dabbled once and all got hooked and it changed completely the face of the criminal justice system.

In the prison heroin market demand outstripped supply and inevitably dozens of new dealers filled the gaps. Only a tiny minority made any profit, the majority worked on it in order to feed their own habits.

This pattern played out throughout every prison in Scotland. When there is not a lot of money being made there is not a lot of struggle over the market so there was no violence between rival dealers like you get on the streets. Violence did explode on a massive scale though. If you are a dealer and you want payment up front for your gear then the customers will simply move on to one of the dozens of other suppliers. Credit must be given and with credit comes fraud. When an addict decides to defraud a psychopath or a sociopath they don't send him a red letter they open him up or they pay another desperate addict a small parcel of drugs for them to do the damage.

Prison populations completely fragmented, friends were scamming then slashing each other. Pretty soon when the plague seized a tight grip of the addicts, the screws maximised their rewards for information system and grassing, which had been kept discreet, became as prevalent as the porridge. Hell got a hell of a lot worse. Where have I heard that phrase before? I think that I've just stolen it, sorry mate.

The biggest surprise to me was the way that the screws were openly showing happiness. They had the smug smiles of the successful. I could not understand, what maniac would ever want to take a seven thousand strong prison population and rather than make any attempt to treat them kindly in an effort to rehabilitate even a modest percentage, you terrorise and torture creating fear and anger and bitterness and In effect make them one hundred times more dangerous than they ever were. Then you devise a way to get ninety percent of them hooked on a drug that is so powerful that most of them will be absolutely locked into a life of crime destruction and addiction. What kind of maniac would do that?

After only a few weeks it had become crystal clear that the mandatory drug testing was a complete disaster and far from curb any drug abuse it had caused a heroin plague to infect the entire prison estate. Yet far from reverse and repair the damage, the SPS made it even worse by aggressively ramping up their drug testing programme.

I was confused amazed angered and eventually awakened. I analysed and studied and tried to work out what was going on. My work on it took almost a year and when I woke up to the truth, the answers that I found were obvious and sickening.

At the top of the heap are the Royals with their power and their wealth how they may have came by it and what lengths they will go to in order to keep a firm grip of it.

There is a very good reason why it is called Her Majesty's prisons and the Crown Office Prosecution Service and Her Majesty's Secret Service and so on. There is a reason for the gruesome machine that is the criminal justice system. It was not created in order to protect you. From its very inception it was created solely as a weapon that would be used to protect the Royals.

If you look back at true history you will see hunter gatherers settling down and farming. Small communities were created and everyone traded with a barter system. It is natural for humans to help each other and everyone did so.

Suddenly out of nowhere came a so called king. He claimed to be the owner of the entire country and he forced everyone to pay rent and tax to him. His warlords even murdered people who dare to eat so much as a rabbit without first paying a tax on it.

Nothing in history gives even a shred of evidence that these kings were legitimate or decent people, the contrary is true. From those days up to these days every successive monarch has committed theft by inheritance and has absolutely refused to give up their power or control or to give back their vast wealth to the descendants of those from whom it was stolen.

There is nothing whatsoever to prove that the Royal family are anything other than a mafia. Traditionally they have destroyed anyone who dared to speak such truth. You would be charged with Treason and judged to be either insane or evil for daring to challenge their fairytale version of history and they would murder you.

If there were only 250 spies and police in Britain and the people learned the truth and subsequently decided to take back the power control and wealth that has been stolen by the royal mafia then the job would be easy and even inevitable. In my mind it is no coincidence that there is so much manufactured crime in Britain that we require 250,000 spies and police. They are all forced to swear an allegiance to the monarch and the royal family not to the good people who pay their wages and who they are allegedly there to protect. The criminal justice army are the secret bodyguard of the royal mafia and are there to protect them from the true owners of the country.

That may explain why none of them seem to be honest or decent people, the top ranks are mostly hand picked brutes and when you look closely at their activities and analyse their characters you will see that they are only there to protect the fake authority and seized power and stolen wealth of the mafia. They view and treat everyone as a suspect and a threat because they work for an illegitimate boss and that does make every decent citizen a threat to them. Their job also entails making sure that you never get to know such truths. This is quite a big thing for most people to accept or even consider and I will expand further with it in chapter five, please try to keep an open mind.

2 Oysters

My jail sentence was coming to an end. Ignorance is bliss as they say and I was certainly toiling a bit now that I could see the bigger picture. Knowledge of the wicked people and their culture made it almost impossible for me to ignore what I had suffered at their hands. I could now understand what lurked behind the cruel look about the eyes and the brutality of most of the screws. They had sold their souls and signed up as slaves. It was clear that they would kill or die for their monarch. A thief. And it was theft on an unbelievably vast scale from the poorest of the poor who had no possible way to recoup the loss.

We cannot have anarchy therefore we must have a criminal justice system. It should be there to represent and protect the people and part of that involves punishing wrongdoers. If the system was fair and just and if the punishment part truly represented the interests of the people then most criminals would at least have the opportunity to reflect and possibly even rehabilitate.

However it is in the interests of the rulers to have as many criminals as possible committing as much crime as they can. That allows the establishment to justify the massive criminal justice army who are predominantly only there to protect the power and wealth of the monarchy rather than protect the public.

While we remain in the dark regarding our true history we will continue to be victimised by every part of their system. The most destructive part of that is the manufactured crime waves and mass imprisonment in brutal illegitimate prisons. The regimes themselves are a horrific form of psychological torture and are very damaging and debilitating. I suffered it for almost two years and like most other victims of that machinery I asked 'that was all for what?' In my case it was one punch to the head and a bit of pepper spray to a bouncer and one fight with a skinhead. The screws did ten times more damage than that every day of the week every week of the year and unlike me they were not provoked. They choose the victims at random simply in order to practice a reign of terror.

I had committed crimes and I was due punishment but this,

by these roasters. No one deserves that. Thankfully I could now see and understand that they fully intended for us to recognise the injustice. They were literally trying to drive us mad forcing us into a rage because we were their bread and butter so they felt the need to do absolutely everything in their power to guarantee so much outrage and anger in the minds of the prisoners that re-offending would come automatically and that would guarantee future work and justification for the vast army of state employees.

I could now see the true depths of the game and I wanted to stay out of it. I vowed that I would no longer let anger cloud my judgement. I would redouble my efforts to avoid violent conflict. If someone was in desperate need of my help then I would provide it. However I would make the conscious effort to ignore all of the sparks that used to attract me and I would only ever take action in future if it was the last possible resort.

Freedom was coming. I had not ordered any new books for a couple of weeks so I re-read an old favourite 'Shogun' by James Clavell. If you are ever in jail then you must read that book. It takes you deep into ancient Japan and into the Samurai culture. Ultimate freedom for a lonely prisoner starved of sensory stimulation.

My last couple of days I spent with Captain Von Beck in 'The War Hound and The Worlds Pain' by Michael Moorcock. That wonderful book had first presented itself to me when I was just 13 years old. Every time that I read it I am reminded of how the young teenage me had interpreted and enjoyed that story. Mr Moorcock I thank you with all of my heart, you brought the first taste of word magic to me. Thank you.

In Barlinnie I used the book to get me through the last evening. Lots of prisoners get gate fever but I was alright and later that night I managed to sleep soundly. They actually had to wake me up in the morning.

Freedom. The long walk to the main gate was exciting yet I was still reasonably calm. I reached the gate, answered a few questions and BANG! Suddenly I was a free man and what an amazing feeling after nearly two years of physical incarceration and psychological torture.

My mind was swimming in amazing chemicals far stronger than any drug that I have ever heard of. It is an amazing feeling of euphoria and is almost impossible to describe fully. I was taken straight up for some of my mum's good food. It was a beautiful experience to see my loved ones in friendly surroundings with no malevolent screws staring at us. After too long in hell I was now in a home filled with love. I sat down on the couch and was amazed as I sank into the softness of a proper seat. Next came the almost forgotten sensations of hot food and metal cutlery, it was all really strange and was a unique sort of trip.

Most of the torture of imprisonment that I suffered is confined to a hazy blur in my memory. Unfortunately the delightful experience of suddenly being free from torture was so overwhelming that it too has become a hazy blur, although this one is beautiful and full of love.

While I had been locked up I had not been able to earn. There is no situation that would prevent me from earning once I was released so during my time in jail I had given every penny of my savings away to friends and family whenever any of them had needed it during the period.

The summer of 1996 was just leaving as I returned to freedom. After enjoying the company of my family I decided to resume the partying. I was still attracted to labels back then and when my friend gifted me a wage I went straight to the clothes shops Cruise and Versace to get some stuff.

I had a haircut, went home to change then hit the pubs with my friend the Ton. Like a mug I drank heavy and never even got a bird. Nearly two years without any and I bounce up the road drunk. What a loser. The next day we went to Partick met two friends and eventually landed in a pub. We ended up visiting almost every pub in Partick then Byres road then Ashton Lane, drunk again. I never realised it at the time but looking back now I was using beer to dull the pain that I was feeling after suffering the horrific experience that is imprisonment.

After a few days I managed to get back to work. I am a ceramic tiler to trade and am a perfectionist. I love to walk into plain kitchens and bathrooms and turn them into ceramic works of art. When I see the joy on our customers faces I feel a glow. The wages are just a by product for me, my main incentive is the buzz that I get from making peoples homes look beautiful.

My dad learned the trade in the 1950's and apart from a barren spell in the 70's he had solid work. He taught it to me in the 80's. He is the original perfectionist and was only ever focused on bringing delight to customers. He kept prices as reasonable as possible and devoted every waking hour to the job. He never took one holiday in 50 years.

No adverts, never any complaints and hardly ever a dry month. Such is the result of good recommendations from happy customers. My dad did most of his work for free by passing on our trade discount to the customers. The majority of them saved more money from the price of the materials than they spent on paying us. We could have pocketed all of that money and doubled our earnings however we are not in it for the pay and that would be a snide move anyway.

My dad loves it when I do the good work but he has been disappointed by my thirst for danger in the past and the resulting imprisonment that I have suffered. He is a supremely intelligent man and I don't doubt that it hurts him to see his son acting like a brain dead monkey. I have tried to make it up to him and my mum in other ways in an effort to ease their disappointment.

I had been free for a couple weeks when I received a call from an old customer. His restaurant had been completely gutted. The insurance company were going to pay for a total refurbishment. I went along to measure up the kitchen. It was a good big job, the problem was that he was waiting for a cheque to come in and could I supply the materials. No problem. I borrowed some money from my dad and the remainder from a guy who I thought was alright. The materials cost me quite an amount and I did the job in good time working hard and late into every evening. Even though it was a commercial job I still worked to perfection. I have never been a bread head tiler who just wants to batter up tiles all day to cover the mortgage and the motor.

When I finished and packed up my tools to go, the customer was nowhere to be seen. I phoned, no answer, I left a message. There were a few painters still on the job doing the front end so I also left word with them for the customer to phone me. Days soon turned into weeks and I got more desperate and angry as time went on. I was out of pocket for a healthy amount and I was beginning to get pretty mad. I started to appear at the site trying to catch him and eventually I did. He apologised and explained that he was skint, he had tanked his savings on the refurbishment and had run out before he could even buy the materials for the kitchen never mind pay me. That is why he had asked me to do a supply and fix deal on it. He told me that the insurance company would only pay him once all works were finished and passed.

I wasn't sure if that was true. He had no way of knowing that I had not been earning for almost two years and was just as skint as him. If his problems had come from gambling or drugs or such then I would not have been pleased. As it happens his was honest poverty and he was after all only trying to do some work to provide for his family. I forgave him and told him that I was struggling myself and asked if he would pay me as soon as he could.

That was it. The touch of fate that would begin my next powerful experience in the game of life. I was in a bad way. It was hard enough trying to get over the agony of imprisonment and trying to readjust. And where I had been right up on top before I went to jail I was now scratching my arse through empty pockets.

It all became too much to put up with and I became involved in a robbery. The job was a jewellers in Perth 65 miles to the north east of Glasgow. The prize was a cabinet full of Rolex watches.

I was introduced to Mr N he turned out to be a great guy with a funny sense of humour but at first sight he is a frightening individual. He would provide the transport, would act as the getaway driver and would watch my back while I worked in the shop. The robbery was not a professional job it was basic and simple using our aggressive presence to get the goods and a race against the clock to outrun the police response. In short it was a high risk quick earner.

We drove all of the way to Perth. I was in a Nissan and Mr N was in a Ford. Just before we reached the town I passed a large petrol tanker. It was sunny and had been raining, the spray from the tanker's wheels swept up onto the bonnet of my stolen Nissan as I passed and the sunlight created a small rainbow which came right onto the car. I took it as a good omen and was happy that I was about to collect a wee pot of gold.

Off the main route and into traffic. My nerves started. I had only been free for 56 days and if you read one thousand crooks books they will all warn you against ever working with anyone who is fresh out of jail. Bad luck is believed to follow them out. In my opinion it is the negative energy and the debilitated spirit that affects the performance of the ex-con. Incidentally that bad luck is believed to last for anything up to five years after release. I had no need to worry about such things because like every other optimistic person on earth I believe that I am unique and will not suffer the same fate as anyone who has gone before.

None of the other motorists even glanced at me. I looked just like every other salesman, wearing suit trousers a bright crisp white shirt a nice blue tie and a bored facial expression.

Mr N and I stopped our cars side by side in a car park at the top of a hill that could not be seen from the quiet road nearby. It was too far away from the jewellers and also was not a clever choice due to the giant hill however the secluded spot so close to the town made me ignore the negatives and focus solely on the positive. Not normally a wise move. The Nissan was to be our second car so I left it and dressed up with a long ski jacket over my clothes, I carried my mask in my pocket and jumped in beside Mr N in the Ford.

He was buzzing and his excitement infected me and gave me an instant rush of fear and adrenaline. High stakes bring masses of emotions. We had never met before being introduced the other night and that is a loss because such situations can require the telepathic communications that grow between people who are close.

I zipped up to my neck then lifted my empty (soon to be full) sports bag. I looped the strap over my head and shoulder then tugged at both clips to double check that it was secure. Whoosh! A massive rush of adrenalin screamed through my body like liquid lightning. Amazing. I pulled my leather gloves down tighter onto my hands. Lets go. Mr N drove off as I lifted a brand new sharp brick hammer and placed it into my bag which was now resting on my lap.

The residential roads were deserted in this small suburb on the edge of the town centre. Mr N drove down the hill in silence. We were both very alert to absolutely every sight and each wave of energy in the air.

If you are ever in a car with a traffic police driver then you will notice the strange way that they drive, very precise and a bit nervous from masses of skills tests. If you are ever in a car with a getaway driver then you will see that they also have a strange driving style only this one is far more relaxed and at the same time dominant and a bit aggressive from years of high speed chases and rallying joyrides in other peoples cars. Mr N had that strange getaway driver style and it was very comforting to be in such safe hands. I could tell instinctively that he would not shy away from an absolute full speed demolition derby if that is what was required to get us home for our tea tonight.

We crept down the steep hill. Mr N had his big jacket on and had his mask ready. Our collective energy was swirling around the inside of our car in waves of madness and caused my body temperature to shoot up and the sweat to break out on my skin. An amazing combination of fear excitement adrenalin and determination.

I felt for sure that there was nothing that Mr N could not beat or demolish on the road and I was so fired up that there was nothing that could stop me on the pavements. The prize was ours, we just had to go and collect it.

Mr N handed me the police scanner which had been sat in between his legs. It being Perth there was not much chatter and I had to check the screen to make sure that it was on. I placed the scanner inside my bag facing up the way and with the volume up full.

This is it. Red light stop. Whoosh! More adrenalin chasing the last wave along. Tunnel vision, bright white route ahead, sides fading from grey to black. Determination. Explosive energy millimetres under the manufactured calm exterior. Amber, green we're off! Mr N glides the Ford perfectly along, right turn, over bridge, travel round the narrow streets on the one way system. Scan the entire area, no threats, listen to the police scanner, no chatter, slow down left turn coming up. Whoosh! Absolutely staggering mix of powerful emotions. Turn left, here we go! It's time for mayhem. Heart is hammering rapidly, thump-thump-thump heavy breathing thump-thump-thump control it. Keep eyes focused. Continuously scanning for danger. One lane, no traffic, target two hundred metres ahead. Danger! Traffic warden, he has radio contact straight to the police. What to do? Fortune favours the bold. Too risky to follow the one way system all the way round again. Lets just do it. Onwards. Target one hundred metres ahead. Screaming adrenalin electrifying my entire body. Head exploding with crackling energy. Bright white road up ahead to target, pavements grey, shops and buildings fade to black, pedestrians, black – no danger in sight. Search the air for evil energy, none - no police around. Mr N is breathing heavy, his massive shoulders and chest are heaving up and down, straining against the seatbelt. Target fifty metres ahead. Last scan for danger. All senses on absolute maximum alert. All clear. Mask on, the time is now! Mr N hits his seatbelt release button and flicks it off expertly. Target in range. Whoosh! Absolutely electric surge of atomic energy. Mr N slows car down BOOM! A massive sledgehammer blow of fear slams into my solar plexus as I reach the point of no return. I force my way through the uncomfortable wave with gritted teeth. Mr N hits his wave of fear at the point of no return and I actually hear the air being forced out of his lungs. What a buzz! He drives two metres too far. "Stop! Stop here!" I call and he hesitates. I grab the handbrake on and we stop two metres past our point. Our car is now blocking the road. Here we go! The boom crack and clatter of an adrenalin thunderstorm is crashing throughout my entire body. Check the road, clear. Check the pavement, covered in about twenty shoppers none of them are a threat. Half a dozen are standing looking into the very window display that I'm after. They are in for a show. Jump out of the car. Sprint round it, sprint straight across road and pavement. Leap into the air at full speed. Bang! I smash my foot into the wooden frame of the glass door and it crashes in giving me an opening. Hand in bag. Extract brick hammer. Half step in door, left turn. Moving too fast to even see anything or anyone inside shop. Security glass. Swing hammer full force cricket bowl Crash! Grab thick curtain snatch it out of the way. All mid level watches hard to sell, leave them. An unseen partition. Security glass beside. Swing hammer again Crash! Grab this curtain snatch it away Prize! Rolex cabinet. Three sides thick glass, wooden doors at back facing me. Swing hammer small arcs this time Crack! A chunk flies out exposing unvarnished wood underneath.

The doors buckle an inch. Spread feet into boxer stance for power Crack! Crack! Crack! Crack! Crack! Open! Hammer back into bag. Mr N appears at doorway to my left. He is roaring at shop workers, I don't know why, Are they coming towards my back? No time to turn around and check. He's pointing a gun at them now, he never mentioned a gun to me. The size of him he doesn't need a gun. Too late to worry now. Get the prize. Snatching Rolex watches and feeding them to my hungry bag. Flick my eyes up to see the amazed faces of the window shoppers who are mesmerised by the show. The thick front window of the shop keeping them safe from the tantalisingly close theatre of robbery. "Lets go! Lets go! Lets go!" I look to my left again and Mr N is roaring at me. I only have 13 watches. There are still some in the cabinet and I want a go at the diamond display in the other window. "Lets go! Lets go!" He takes a backwards step to the doorway and lowers his gun. Maybe he has seen some danger. Cant tell. This will have to do. Must go. I nod and spin towards him. He flies out the door. I follow without ever looking at the inside of the shop or the people we have just frightened. Rush over pavement. Across road into car. Away!

CCTV footage would later show that the entire thing lasted 61 seconds. Mr N speeds us forwards expertly. My job is done. He screamed us round the first corner. A wail from the engine echoed up the tall buildings.

"I never knew you had a gun. You are frightening enough on your own mate." I said as I began to calm down. "It's a replica. Did anyone jump on your back?" He asked. Point taken.

Right turn and I'm pushed into the door from the force. Seatbelt on. Left turn across bridge engine roaring. Lift police scanner, massive amount of chatter. All excited screaming from them. Probably the first robbery in Perth since the days of Wallace.

Hard left turn flying up the hill towards blind bend with a high hedge. Check the prize, not bad for one minutes work. Round blind bend. We screech to a sudden halt. Road is blocked by a turf truck and a big lorry. What's the chances.

"The coppers are behind us!" Mr N suddenly informs me. I look out of the back window and cant see over the high hedge. "Why didn't you tell me before?" I said. "Is it armed response or ordinary coppers?" I ask worried. "Don't know." He answers nonchalantly. He seemed to be in joyrider mode where a police chase is all part of the fun. I was in robber mode where police could be the murderous coward armed response mob.

We could not drive back without meeting the police. "We have to bail here and try to run." I said as I snatched my door open. We leaped out of the car and I was weighed down with the bag the hammer the scanner and the watches. Thirteen oysters. An aphrodisiac today for sure. We ran up the hill at each side of the lorry. After just a few steps the steep hill was battering the life out of my thigh muscles.

Note to self, never ever park your second car up a hill you clown. I came round the front of the lorry just in time to see Mr N in full reservoir dogs mode. There was a nice wee lady sat in a VW polo waiting for the lorry and the truck to move and let her drive down the hill. Mr N and I were still fully masked up.

He caught sight of me in his peripheral vision just as he was beginning to raise his replica gun to point it at the lady and steal her car. I read it rapidly and caught him short. "Leave her!" I roared. His entire body conveyed his amazement. "You'll give her a heart attack she doesn't know what we want leave her alone!" I ran past him and the VW to emphasise my point.

I wasn't happy with threatening the shop workers with a gun and to this day I still feel guilty about the fright that we must have given them. I hoped that they had the intelligence to know that robbers rob people, it's normally only killers who kill people so if you stand back and obey any orders then you will not normally be harmed by robbers. It is a bit of a fright but you are safe if you behave yourself. So no real need to fear robbers.

This woman in the car was a different thing entirely. If we took her car then there is no doubt that we would escape no problem. But at what cost? I could never frighten a vulnerable person, she had no possible way of knowing what we were about and would have every reason to believe that we intended to hurt her. I would never do that and I would never let anyone else do it. Never have and never will. I would rather go to jail.

If it had been an able bodied young man then I would not have hesitated for a second I would have taken his car and if he resisted then I would have cracked his chin. As it happened it was a woman so I would never dream of it.

The workers from the lorry and the truck thought that we were some sort of bag snatchers and instinctively started running up the hill behind us. I stopped and turned to Mr N "Check this mob." He immediately turned to face them, "Get on the floor you fucking bams move get down now do it down now!" He roared like a madman and I was impressed. He really is a formidable character.

It was immediately clear to the workmen that we were something very different to junkie bag snatchers and they all stopped on the spot. We were off again and carried on running up the hill. The thing was so steep that our full pace sprint was like the standstill slow motion running that you get in a nightmare. Mr N looked over to me, "How far away is the motor?" He asked feeling the lung crushing gradient and praying that the car was not as far away as he could remember. The trouble is that it was.

After what seemed like miles and minutes we reached the entrance of the driveway to a monastery. The police scanner suddenly informed me that they had eyes on us. I looked back and there was a police car away down where the truck had moved away to let them get past.

We could not carry on directly towards the second car now so we branched right and ran down the driveway towards the monastery. It was a respite from heading up that brutal hill. We ran through the small car park then jumped over a wall and ran down a path through some trees.

Using the building as cover we then began heading back up the hill towards the second car. It got steeper as we went along and eventually we were forced to walk. Just trying to breathe was agony. It was as if the oxygen was up at two hundred degrees. Our throats and lungs were on fire and in screaming pain.

Even although we were shattered the second car was now only two hundred metres up this hill and the scanner told us that the police believed that we were hiding behind the monastery. There was a back road down off this hill so we were home free.

I was completely exhausted and gave Mr N the bag to carry for a while. We were both wheezing like ninety year old lung cancer victims soaked with sweat and knackered.

We were labouring up the last part of the hill breathing deep rapid agonising breaths and moving on pure adrenalin. There was a row of trees up in front of us then a path only about four steps wide then thick woods and beyond about eight trees deep was our car. It was time to relax and get off home.

After struggling up through the first group of trees we reached the path. Only one step onto the path and I happened to look up to the left. Along the end there was a piece of grass then another road that went down to the monastery.

A police car just happened to be passing on it's way down to where they believed that we were hiding and the passenger just happened to look up and see us. They quickly slammed on their brakes and skidded towards the end of the lane. Both of them jumped out and started up towards us creeping slowly with only coshes in their hands.

We couldn't walk away never mind run. We were completely spent. I looked at Mr N and he shrugged his shoulders in a dejected manner. I was gutted and had to roar at the heavens (whoever that may be, Mother Nature?). I pulled off my mask and looked up at the white sky. I had done wrong of course but this turn of fate was painful.

My words were staggered in between my agonised red hot breathing. "Ive – only – been – out – for – fifty – six – days!" I pulled off my gloves and dropped them on the ground. "Why – are – you – sending – me - back – to – jail?" I pulled off my jacket and quickly untied my tie and ripped it off not wishing to be choked to death by the approaching coppers. Mr N took off his jacket gloves and mask. He then sat down on the ground exhausted. I quickly unbuttoned my shirt and ripped it off and stood there in my t shirt. "What – am – I – meant – to – learn – this – time – eh?" I roared up at the sky.

The two police were close now. "Calm down son." They had been brave enough to approach two robbers who they believed had a real handgun. Im sure that they did not expect to find one roaring up at god like some religious nutcase.

I looked over to them and gestured with my hands, "keyzees – lads – we – are – shattered." I said between heavy breaths.

"Get your hands behind your back!" One shouted and Mr N rolled over onto his front with his hands at the back. I lay down and did the same, we got the obligatory knee in the neck and then the handcuffs were rattled onto our wrists. I was glad of the rest laying there with my mouth wide open. Feed me oxygen.

They gave the good news over the police radio and within a minute there were sixteen of them standing round us. One of the new arrivals picked up the sports bag and looked inside, his growing smile confirmed the contents to his pals.

They split us up and drove us back through the town and into Perth police station. They were processing Mr N first and held me at the desk still cuffed. While I stood there they took my shoes. I was processed then strip searched and given a paper jumpsuit then taken along a corridor and locked in a cell. The cell door slamming shut ended a part of my life. I lay down exhausted physically and emotionally. I had really messed up this time.

I tried to work out what I was meant to learn from this. I had already realised the true nature of the system and I had vowed never to be food for it again, yet here I was serving myself up on a great big plate.

I thought of my Mum and Dad and I had to hold back the tears. They had suffered the torture of seeing me locked up in a hellhole jail for nearly two years and here after only 56 days of freedom I was looking at untold further years of imprisonment.

I would crack anyone who gave my parents any grief whatsoever yet I myself was the cause of their grief, their agony. What could I do? Clearly it would be counter productive to harm myself, was that it? I have to fix myself? I have to change my entire way of thinking. The violence is not the only problem, it is the reckless attitude chasing danger regardless of the potential consequences.

I was 25 years old and it was time for me to grow up. I had enjoyed some wild times but now here I was caught again and that was torturing my loved ones and me. It was not on. It was time to put the brain dead monkey to sleep.

The cruel eyed CID had tried to question us a couple of times but we refused to talk, why help people who are only interested in doing you further harm? They asked us to give mouth swab samples of our DNA. They were asking rather than taking so why give them anything if you have a choice? On Saturday the hatches on our cell doors were all opened and I could hear the food trolley coming round, it stopped at Mr N's door and I heard his muffled voice then a woman as she giggled and gave short answers. Pressing my head to the door I could just peer out and caught sight of her giving Mr N extra food then a cup of tea and he mumbled something else and she giggled again and filled a whole cup with the milk that was only meant for tea so he was doing well. She was not a copper of course so consorting was allowed.

It was now Sunday, we were due up at court tomorrow morning and it would be an automatic remand for such a serious crime. They had not leathered us yet and I was beginning to think that Perth police are a bit more civilised than the Strathclyde division.

They came to my door mob handed. "All that we want is a mouth swab sample of your DNA we have the right to take it without your consent. We wont be using a mouth swab for that, we will be forced to rip hairs out from underneath your arm pits to get the DNA from the follicles." He said. They were all fired up ready to strike. It was clear that they would get the DNA one way or the other and I believed that I had nothing to hide, it would not affect me in any way to give them a sample so I did. That sample would come back to haunt me.

I heard them going along to Mr N's door. There were some muffled voices then a distinctive Crack! and it kicked off. I could hear all the grunting and shouting and howls of pain and could almost see the fight in my mind. He is a solid lad and it took them a couple of minutes to get him down even though there were five of them. At the end it went really strange with inhuman screams and the shout, "Bastard animals!" Later I learned that they had indeed ripped the hairs out from underneath his arms.

Some seconds later I heard Mr N calling for me. "Big yin." He called. He had obviously been knocked unconscious and was now dragging himself over to his cell door. His voice was getting louder. "Big yin. You there?" His voice was loud now. "I'm here." I answered. "Listen for them coming! They got me the bastards, listen for them coming!" He said. "OK mate." I answered. I didn't have the heart to tell him that I had reasoned that they were getting the DNA one way or the other so why get leathered for no reason.

Now that I know him well I realise that he would prefer to get battered every time rather than give anything to the police. Good on you mate. He did give me some stick later on when I confessed to my heinous crime of not taking a beating!

The next day we were taken to Perth Sheriff court separately. We met up in the holding cell underneath it. We couldn't say much because we were surrounded by strangers and all strangers are grasses unless they can prove otherwise. That is the best way to view fellow prisoners if you want to survive.

If a straight person wants to help the police with information then I cant judge them by my moral codes. Criminals who give information are completely different. They don't do it as any sort of moral stance, they do it to help themselves. They harm their comrades by helping their enemy and in my book they are the lowest form of life. They are disgusting creatures. Later on I will expand on what is so wrong with the rewards for information programme.

After a quick court appearance we were remanded in custody. It was off to jail for us. Here I go again. Another excruciating experience in this lifetime. Some say that we choose such things before we come. I wonder then who spiked me with an acid while I was choosing!

3   Lessons Don't Come Cheap

I had to grit my teeth and pull myself together. My taste of freedom had been so brief that my mind was spinning from the shock of this painful twist of fate. I vowed that I would never again feel this agony. My next walk into freedom would be some years off in the future now and I was determined to never repeat this pattern.

The short journey from court to jail was surprising. H.M.P. Perth is literally on the edge of the town. We were taken into a holding tank in the reception area and my surprise grew when I took in the relaxed atmosphere. It was nothing like the hellhole Barlinnie.

We were taken through to 'C' hall. They left us standing at the front desk and I was amazed at the spectacle. The screws all looked like normal human beings, not one of them had the perverted fake gangster growl that hangs off the face of the majority of the Barlinnie mob. They issued us with some essentials and sent us up to the 3rd flat. They had made us both Strict Escapee prisoners so we could not be kept on the top flat with the remand prisoners in case we dug out through the roof. C hall had every type of prisoner (apart from women unfortunately). Our half of the third flat was mixed full of long and short term prisoners. The other half was caged off for sex offenders and grasses who were on protection. They only got out to play when we were all locked up. The entire hall together was the craziest wing since one flew over the cuckoos nest.

As we walked up the stairs I stopped and looked at Mr N. "These are almost as steep as that bastard hill eh." We laughed at the agony. "I'm sorry mate, I should never have picked that spot for a change over. I don't know what I was thinking, I'm an eejit." I said feeling guilty for getting Mr N caught down to my sheer stupidity.

"Forget it." Mr N said. He was raging at me however he had the decency to realise that I was sorry and I would be paying dearly for the mistake. Unfortunately so would he.

Up on our flat we were greeted by the passman, he knew Mr N. They were both from the same district in the east end of Glasgow. We all piled into his cell and two more Eastenders came in, Mr N told them a quick version of the story right up to the part where he was leathered by the police.

"They charged me with assault on five coppers!" He said angrily. "They boot fuck out of me then charge me with assault. They've also charged me with threatening the workers on the hill and the woman in the car." He said. "They've hit me with the same except the police assaults." I said. I was not happy with the added charges but what can you do? Prosecutors are a law unto themselves in Britain.

We were looking at heavy jail time for this. I borrowed some phone cards called my family and assured them that I was alright and would book them a visit. I could feel their pain through the phone and the memory causes me agony to this day. I have been selfish in the past. I try to tell myself that my character was made that way in order to bring me the experiences and lessons that I must learn during this current lifetime. How else can I live with the pain that I have brought upon my loved ones in the past each time that I've been sent to jail.

It could be that my theory about fate is simply a survival mechanism. Equally it could be argued that my journeys to the farthest reaches of the human experience coupled with my inquisitive nature have provided me with the gift of vision and that I have stumbled upon truths that would otherwise be almost impossible to grasp.

My theory does require an open mind and a stretch of the imagination but it makes sense. The alternative is pure chaos and that makes no sense, the question why becomes too big in the face of pure chaos. And the evidence from all corners of the world throughout every century lends weight to something more than chance at work and it could just prove the theory of fate and evolution through learning. Some teachers believe that we find the answers once we pass into the spirit world where our intellect and consciousness are not confined inside the limited capacity of the human brain and are not held back by the human condition. Is it too late by then? Perhaps. Should we seek the answers here and now? Definitely.

I slept briefly that night and the next morning I was bewildered at the workings of the hall. The drug tests had caused a heroin plague in here just like every other jail. The screws in Perth had sat right back and let the prisoners run wild with heroin. The place was full of needles so instead of the buzzing junkies who burn the smack and run about talking shite all day, this hall had the shop doorway mob all literally flopping about everywhere, either half asleep or half dead. I had to step over a guy on the stairs who was turning blue and no one cared. To see this sort of craziness in a jail bolstered all of my previous conclusions about the justice system.

Delight came when I found a large well stocked library. As an escapee I had one screw with me wherever I went and he had a book with my photo and details inside and he had to get it signed off whenever he handed me over to the next screw. A massive waste of time and money. We had no intentions of escaping. They had only put us on it presumably because they had never had such a crime or such prizes caught up here.

One day a large delivery had just come into the library with boxes and boxes of books. I dived in like a wee boy at Christmas and found some good ones. A comedian in the charity shop where the books had been sent from had slipped in a cracker, the SAS Escape and Evasion manual. It was all about escaping from camps. It taught you how to pick locks, get through fences, get over sharp wire and many more tricks. I stifled my laughter and took it straight to the personal guard who was being paid to prevent me from escaping. I smiled and handed him the book.

"That's a good one eh?" I asked. He nodded innocently and handed it back without really looking at it. Every warder in the world is lazy that is why they go for such a no use feet up bogus job in the first place. He was too lazy to even read the title. When I handed it to the library passman his eyebrows shot up at seeing a strict escapee prisoner who had just found an escape and evasion book. It had not been put on his files yet and he gave it back to me without listing it.

The library became my favourite spot. I read books constantly however my escapee status started taking a serious toll on me. The nightshift had to check Mr N and me every fifteen minutes. Our cells were directly opposite each other. The screws would open the spy-hole on the cell door with a loud metallic Clack! And would put the light on in the cell to check that I was in. They would then slam the spy-hole cover back down with another loud Clack!

Those checks were done every fifteen minutes for the next Seven Months into the future. I could not get into a deep sleep and was only ever able to catch fourteen-minute naps before being shocked awake again. It was sleep deprivation and was torture. Eventually I managed to force a piece of plastic into my spy-hole cover and wedged it permanently open. It meant that the screws could now sneak up and look in whenever they liked and being bored and nosey they all did regularly. I was still being woken up every fifteen minutes with the checks but at least I was not being shocked awake with a fright. Mr N also eventually had enough and he got a piece of metal and ripped the cover off the spy-hole on his cell door.

The entire jail was run as a nut house. Like Barlinnie there was no attempt at rehabilitation or anything remotely like it. The opposite was true. There was an education department but it was small and hard to get into. The other prisoners found it much easier to get into heroin and day dream the days away in a stupid fog of drunkenness.

On a par with every other British prison there was never an empty cell. One guy would move out and that very day the bus from court would bring the next victim who would be moved into the cell while the stained mattress was still warm and the stinking cloud from the roll up smoke had not yet cleared. Full capacity equals maximum profits.

Our indictments came in and we were amazed to see that they had dropped the charges regarding the workmen and the woman in the VW polo. It made no sense at first. Why would a prosecutor take something off? They normally add charges on. We were not complaining of course, we were happy to be facing less time. It was impossible to understand. Every prosecutor exaggerates the charges to make everything worse for the accused. This one had done the opposite. Some weeks later we got the answers when the witness statements came in. Every workman had stated that they heard me shouting at Mr N to leave the woman alone. And none of them had mentioned that they had been frightened by him. So that was it. The prosecutor had an allergic reaction to evidence that would show that I was decent enough to help the woman even at the cost of my freedom. That information had no business being aired in a courtroom. A criminal with a heart and some decency, Never!

It was so alarming to him that he would literally prefer to hit us with less charges which would get us lighter sentences as bad men than let the truth come out and get us heavier sentences with me at least being shown as not so bad. Such is the apparently deranged and perverted perspective of a practitioner of the black art of Scots law.

Glasgow high court was being refurbished at that time so every high court sitting was being spread about the sheriff courts. We were given a date for an appearance in Aberdeen. Life went on as we waited for D day.

There were plenty of interesting characters in Perth jail. I became friendly with one guy M. He had been a professional armed robber with some large results to his name. Luck had run out and he was sentenced to ten years for a big job worth a lot of money. He did the time and after his release he went back to work too soon. He was nicked again on a job that was not as big as the first but it got him another ten year sentence thanks to the fact that the first ten years had not cured him. After the second sentence was over he knocked it all on the head and embraced the quiet life. One night he believed that he may have been in a spot of bother. Later he bumped into an old friend and mentioned the perceived problem and just by pure chance the friend had an armed robbery on the go the next day. He did not need another body but he offered M a place on the team as a favour and a way to earn a few quid and get away for a while. M ignored his instincts and agreed to do the work. The very next day they did the job and it came on top. There was an armed siege and they had some fun telling the police that they wanted curries and such. It ended up live on tv and they eventually came out of the bank with their hands in the air and sadness on their faces. It was in Anniesland near my house in Temple. I had watched it on the news and here I was all these years later talking to one of the robbers.

M was sentenced to fifteen years for just that one robbery on account of his bad previous convictions. I cant remember exactly but I believe that he never got any time off on parole and had to do ten soul destroying years in jail.

Another interesting character was big H. He too was an armed robber. A nosey neighbour had seen him do a car changeover and the police had arrested him for one job. They then found a further twenty-three robberies that were similar to the one that H had done. By charging him with them all they got to clear their books of all of those unsolved crimes. Evil people. If he got a bad jury and was convicted of all of that work then he would be killed dead with a sentence of twenty years or so. Luckily the jury were intelligent enough and only came back with a guilty verdict for the one job that he had done. The judge must have been upset at not being able to slaughter H for all of the crimes that he had not done so he gave him ten years for the one robbery that would normally result in five years.

H was an intelligent guy and it was a tragedy what had been inflicted upon him. He used to speak about his agony at missing his kid growing up. I think it was a girl or maybe it was one boy and one girl. I cant remember exactly. He ended up being refused parole and then had three years added onto his sentence. By the time he was due for release he had suffered nine long years of torture. There was a good ending though. While he had been inside, the national lottery had started and he had never been able to play it of course. He used to talk about it all the time and a few guys mentioned the strange topic of conversation. None of us could play it so no one was interested.

Two weeks after he was released a newspaper headline read, "Should this armed robber get to keep the money?" He had won two million. He must have been having premonitions about it and that is why he spoke of it so often. He paid a heavy debt for one robbery so it was nice to see fate pay him something back. Not enough but help none the less.

In every jail the majority of the population have suffered some degree of injustice. Don't believe the Hollywood myth which tells you that every prisoner claims to be innocent. The majority are guilty and they admit it and even accept injustices such as exaggerated charges or perjury, myth and other dirty tricks from the prosecution. Also extra long sentences on the whims of some judges. Most prisoners accept such things and quietly pay their debt to society.

Please don't believe the Hollywood propaganda spinners when they try to tell you that every accused is guilty and is the bad guy and is always claiming to be innocent. They tell you all of those lies because as members of the public you are the jurors of tomorrow. Cynical and paranoid jurors are perfect tools for a legal system to manipulate. That is why they try to use propaganda.

There are guilty people trying to tell lies but it is not as big a thing as you have all been led to believe. Please keep an open mind if you are ever on a jury. Try not to be cynical or paranoid. Stay wide awake.

Inside our jails there are also a sickening amount of victims of absolute injustice. Innocent people are stitched up and locked up, usually for life. Most of you have seen a few true horror stories of injustice made into films like 'The Hurricane' or 'In the name of the father'. It is not just in the few cases that have made it onto film. Time and again the establishment does absolutely everything in its power in order to deny justice to innocent people. The victims are forced to battle for decades in order to win their fight for freedom. That way the fiends can explain away the 'mistakes' by saying that these sorts of miscarriages of justice all happened decades ago and there are plenty of safeguards to prevent them from happening these days.

Every time that someone eventually wins their battle for justice the spin doctors use the same excuses and in twenty years time those same lies will be repeated regarding the victims of injustice who are suffering today and it will still serve to keep the public blind to the culture of malevolence that is at the heart of the system.

It is a disease and is almost impossible to beat. That is why you only ever hear about a tiny percentage of victims of injustice. The majority either die off or are exhausted from battering their faces against the concrete wall of corruption for so many years that they die internally and give up.

Like every jail in Britain, Perth had plenty of injustice victims. It takes very strong and determined individuals to stay the course and manage to battle the forces of darkness for extended periods. People with the will to fight ferociously for years and years are a rare breed. In Perth jail there were a few. While I was there two in particular fought harder than the rest. They were JD and JS.

JD had been found near the scene of a bank robbery. The robbers were long gone and when the police questioned JD if he had seen anything he told them that he was Connor McLeod the Highlander (from the movie). Clearly he had problems. Unlucky for him he had ran into the wrong police that day. They arrested him and charged him with the bank job. When it was pointed out that he did not fit the description of the robbers and had no mask or money the police simply said that he must be the getaway driver. How the actual robbers managed to leave their getaway driver at the scene and still get away themselves was never investigated. It was typical of a stitch up and the crown used the full weight of the law in order to convict JD. He was sentenced to six years for a robbery that he had not committed.

His insanity became too much for the prison service so they sent him to the state hospital at Carstairs. He appealed his sentence and it was clear that he had not robbed the bank. He was acquitted and yet he still had to work hard to get back out of Carstairs asylum. Eventually he did win but the sick members of the legal establishment did not want to let him go. It is as if they get some kind of perverted thrill from injustice and from locking up innocent people. They now charged him with having pretended to be insane and again used the full weight of the law against him. The sentence? Six years!

To top it all off they let him know that they were at it all along when they started giving him anti psychotic medication while they had him locked up for six years allegedly for pretending to be in need of such treatment. JD had the clarity to see the injustice and he has a good strong family outside who stood by him and fought for his cause never tiring and never giving up. He fought the establishment all of the way and while I was in Perth he cut his cell bars with a hacksaw and went up on a rooftop protest for New Years night. Not an easy feat in the Perth winter and up on the icy ramparts of the jail halls.

He made it a great night for us because it really boosts the spirit to see a man who has been brutalised and tortured relentlessly by an army yet he still finds the courage and the strength to fight back against all odds.

I cant remember the entire story in detail however I am sure that he never did get the justice that he deserved and was kept in and served the sentence. You can find JD the Highlander in media archives.

The other one was JS. His case may be familiar to you because he was one of the two men who were stitched up and sentenced to multiple life sentences for a mass murder that they had not committed. Their case had come out of the infamous Glasgow ice cream wars. Read the book 'Indictment' for more details.

JS and his co-accused TC fought an amazing war against the establishment for twenty years. TC used hunger strikes and JS used escapes in their collective efforts to highlight their case and let the public know what had happened to them. During their epic battle for justice they were repeatedly brutalised by the legal system and the screws who hate to see men who can take the ultimate torture and still get back up and struggle and fight.

Not long before the rooftop protest by JD there had been the latest escape attempt by JS. He had almost got away and was only caught by a sharp eyed spoil sport who believed that the uniform was real but recognised the face of the screw who was about to walk out of the gate wearing it as the now well known victim of injustice JS. He was rumbled and locked up.

He went on a dirty protest in C hall. That is when a prisoner refuses all orders and covers his cell and himself in shit. It is a disgusting tactic however not even remotely near disgusting as the activities of the establishment against TC and JS. Unfortunately for us his cell was beside the area where we had to collect our food and walk up the stairs. The smell was terrible but we were all behind him completely. Like I said, guilty people admit guilt. Only the genuinely innocent can fight for extended periods. Their innocence gives them the strength to battle on and when they do they normally have the full backing of the jail population.

After almost two whole Decades of war TC and JS smashed it and eventually won their case and were at last proven to be innocent and were set free. As usual none of the monsters who had set them up and denied them justice for all of those years were ever brought to account. Lack of transparency and accountability as always.

Why is it deemed acceptable for members of the establishment to commit such crimes against humanity? Can you imagine the horror if a few perverts were caught with kidnap victims in a horrendous cell where they had been tortured for twenty years? The maniacs would never be released from jail for such a heinous crime. Yet if they first take the time to fill out an application form and are subsequently hired into the establishment then they are automatically immune from any prosecution for any crimes however sick they may be as long as they are committed in the name of the Crown. Why are such things accepted by the people of Britain?

As previously stated there are some malingerers who pretend to be innocent. They are few and far between and are not tolerated. One example was a man who was on remand inside C hall in Perth. He repeatedly told anyone who would listen that he had visited his ex wife and she had then set him up by alleging that he had attacked her. Most prisoners believed him. One day he came back from court having been found guilty and sentenced. The truth came over the radio during the tea time lock up. They said that he was a Hannibal the cannibal beast who had attacked his wife and had even slashed her face. That slashing was his undoing. She clearly had not slashed her own face therefore he was guilty and pretending to be innocent and like a fool he had not joined his brethren in the protection wing.

Everyone hates bullies and there is no worse or more sickening bully than a man who harms a vulnerable person such as a woman or a child. This character did not know that fact and did not know that most of the prisoners could see that any woman could make false allegations against any man however no sane woman would ever slash her own face. So his guilt was clear for everyone to see.

He had been placed on the third flat across the hall from my cell and when our doors were opened back up I had a clear view of the entire six seconds that he lasted before being repeatedly stabbed with a massive jail made dagger. It was more like a sword and made a real mess of him. We later heard that he recovered then killed himself.

Monsters who harm the vulnerable are impossible to understand and nothing frightens quite like the unknown. When they frighten strong men by harming the weak, the men have a natural and powerful urge to put a stop to such behaviour. So take heed anyone who feels the urge to harm the vulnerable, stop yourself now before you end up in some proper trouble. If judges would give such people the sentences that they deserve then no one else would try to balance it up. The judges repeatedly give lenient sentences to evil perpetrators and heavy sentences to proper crooks. I will expand more on sentencing trends later.

Every prisoner feels for the victims of such attacks who have not seen the freaks justly punished and any good strong men who happen to be in jail are only too happy to balance the tally. Hence the carnage and the need for protection halls.

I learned many lessons from a number of people in Perth and was soaking all of it up at every opportunity however I learned the most by far from just one man. LR was a Loyalist paramilitary who had been caught buying machine guns over here on the mainland and shipping them back to Belfast. His story made fortunes for the media as they splashed it all over for weeks after the arrest then again after the court appearance and convictions.

I had always wondered what was truly going on over the water in Ireland and so far I had never been lucky enough to meet someone who knew the truth. In the past I had met one Irish catholic and one Irish protestant on separate occasions but the catholic looked like a grass so I never even spoke to him and the protestant had been shot in the elbows wrists knees and ankles. He said that it was from three separate punishment shootings for stealing cars. Anyone who had not learned that first lesson would have nothing to teach so I never questioned him further.

LR was a different thing entirely. He was intelligent to an unimaginable level. He had a cold alien intelligence. And for reasons that were not at first clear he was keen to make friends with me and that made him loose tongued.

After a few normal friendly conversations I risked enraging him by repeating what I had learned about the history of the royals. I then asked him to educate me about Ireland and the troubles.

Far from get angry he had already seen the true nature of the monarchy. And he had an amazing take on the Irish story. His view was that of a Loyalist paramilitary professional and he told me a great deal. I cant remember the entire story in exact detail and have had to look up relevant dates for accuracy.

The fighting was extensive and complex. He took me back to the battle of the Boyne.

King James was the ruling monarch back then and his unfortunate genetics had come into him and then were passed into his daughter Princess Mary. And also to her cousin Prince William from the Netherlands.

Princess Mary's greed was so desperate that in a disgusting episode she went to bed with her own cousin in order to persuade him to bring his army over and destroy her dad, King James who was Prince William's own uncle. The plan was to kill daddy bear then use the fake justice system to declare his rightful heir and son as illegitimate and allow Princess Mary and her cousin Prince William to steal the inheritance and thus the entire country for themselves.

Prince William agreed and brought his army over to Britain to destroy King James. Holland was a protestant country back then and so the troops who had been forced into Prince William's army had all been brought into that religion. The Dutch also had plenty of wealth from their banking scams. Most of the English gave in and changed sides immediately so King James had to flee to Ireland where he put together an army who happen to have been brought into the catholic religion. The people of both armies were ordinary decent men who were forced to fight in a royal mafia power struggle.

The main battle took place at the river Boyne. Prince William's side won and Princess Mary and him ordered their judges to declare Mary the legitimate heir and to declare her half brother as illegitimate. Once Mary had seized control her husband was crowned King William. It was simply a repeat of numerous occasions when royals had tried to murder each other in order to steal the country from their closest relatives who had themselves stolen it through theft by inheritance.

William was nicknamed King Billy and has been the adopted champion of the Irish protestant cause from that day to this. Yet what was he? A greedy inbred who slept with his own cousin then tried to murder her dad his own uncle then stole the entire country for himself.

The Irish catholic cause had ditched King James for being a loser. Their champion was now the King Pope in Rome and his priest army. Yet what were they? Not as benevolent as their modern counterparts that's for sure.

LR explained to me that the Irish troubles were a war for control over the land of Ireland not the religion. It was a political war which the Queen and the Pope could never lose because they would remain at the top of their respective followers.

Both sides were fighting simply in order to gain control over the parliament where they would have the chance to control the tax spending and they could take care of their own side's priorities first.

The most startling revelation was when he told me that the war was fake. The paramilitaries on the streets were fighting killing and dying in an effort to help their own people but at the top of every terrorist group of both sides was the hand of MI5 who had initiated the war and were playing chess with the warring factions. Behind MI5 of course are the true rulers, the British royal family.

LR's revelations were startling and were made all the better because they confirmed to me many of the theories and conclusions that I had previously come to concerning the true forces of darkness their history and their reptile nature.

During the late fifties and early sixties a civil rights enlightenment spread throughout the planet. A rapid awakening of the people resulted in mass demonstrations demanding freedoms and equal rights worldwide. In 1962 the Irish Republicans renounced violence and declared a ceasefire after 46 years of fighting for a free Ireland. The new wave of enlightenment had woken them up to the fact that Gandhi had been very wise and he realised that when the capitalist system is being run by tyrants they can never be beaten by violence.

In fact when they themselves are subjected to violent attacks they manage to entrench themselves further in and earn out of chaos. They actually need violence and struggles in order to justify their own existence and to persuade everyone that it is not safe to try to go it alone without their war mongering murderous forces to 'protect' you.

When every business starts to lose money they all look up towards the politician puppets of the rulers for answers and solutions. If the rulers cant restore order and get the money machine working again then they are exposed for what they are, useless gangsters who can only rule by force and are in fact not the wisest or the most lucrative option. Peace non-violence and civil disobedience then are the only weapons that will ever beat the tyrants by waking up the masses and showing them the truth and by getting the money men in a panic.

In 1962 faced with a declared ceasefire and a civil rights campaign the British royals ordered MI5 to attack the Irish catholic population on all fronts. Collusion was ramped up massively between the police and the loyalist paramilitaries. Catholics were being burned out of their homes in entire streets and protestant housing officers were ordered not to provide them with proper replacements. The injustices were horrific and were fully intended to get the catholic community to abandon their peaceful approach and to fight back. Violence had failed over the past 46 years though and it was still clear that it was not the way to win.

The atrocities from the police and the loyalists against the catholic people reached such a terrible level that the state could now put their next plan into action and they offered to send over British troops who would protect the innocent victims. Not long after the army were sent over, rogue elements were ordered directly by MI5 to turn around and attack the catholics. LR would not admit to it but the innocent protestants also suffered a great deal. No one was safe.

By 1969 the people had suffered seven long years of horrors and a small group gave in to their anger and returned to arms. The IRA fought back and targeted the nearest perceived enemy, the British troops. Many soldiers were killed yet they were only following orders, they were not the true enemy.

The bulk of the campaigners from the catholic community remained determined to use peaceful means and the rulers had to try harder to enrage this peaceful majority in order to force them to return to violence because while it can kill war, it can never kill peace. A state that only knows how to lie cheat steal oppress manipulate terrorise and kill is rendered useless in the face of peace and disobedience.

The royals did try harder. They suspended the legal system and invented internment. Hundreds of people were locked up indefinitely in prison with no evidence, no charges and no trials. That was still not enough so they began brutalising and torturing the prisoners.

By 1972 after three years of such madness the civil rights campaigners were still fighting peacefully. Terrified and helpless in the face of peace and increasingly exposed as being useless and a waste of funds the rulers ordered troops to fire live rounds straight into hundreds of innocent people who were taking part in a civil rights march. Thirteen of the peaceful protesters were shot dead in what became known as Bloody Sunday. The courts then cleared the shooters of any wrongdoing. The sick tactic worked and the catholic community were so enraged that they put down their peace banners and picked up the guns and the bombs and waged a campaign of violence against an impossible to beat enemy who had finally won the war because they had at last restored the justification for their own existence.

For the next 22 years open warfare on the streets of Northern Ireland ensued. And it even reached the mainland with a determined IRA bombing campaign. The British state loved it. The IRA became the bogey man and were used as an excuse to ultimately put two cameras and three machine gun totting policemen on every main road in the U.K.

The rulers even made sure that the bombing campaign would continue. They did that by fitting up groups of innocent people and jailing them for the mass murders. The two most infamous miscarriages of justice were to become known as the case against the Birmingham Six and the case against the Guildford Four. While the royals wasted tens of millions of taxpayers pounds stitching up trials and convictions against the innocents, the real killers were bombing away to their hearts content. Which of course was the true reason why innocent people were being jailed in order to extend the campaign and the resulting atrocities. They needed the bombing to continue in order to justify turning Britain into a police state that would now be fully equipped and ready to crush under it's boot any civil rights campaigners in the future.

LR's taste of it all as a loyalist had been the witnessing of the widespread collusion and the surprising openness whereby orders would come direct from MI5 to loyalist terror squads and they in turn would go out onto streets cleared of all military and police personnel and they would murder innocent (and sometimes not so innocent) catholics. The police and the military had a hand in it.

One of the worst atrocities occurred on the 12th February 1989 when a loyalist hit squad was ordered to kill the innocent lawyer Pat Finucane. Mr Finucane's crime? He would not collude with the Crown and was actually standing up in court and Defending his clients. A serious criminal offence in the warped minds of our rulers and it was punishable by death according to them. And not a clean death. The team were given very specific orders and they carried them out to the letter. They did not target him at a lonely location, they hit him at home. You would expect them to go in during the night when all potential witnesses were asleep but they had been ordered to crash in during the evening when all the family would be home and awake. An absolute outrage. They smashed in and shot him ten times in the face and head while his terrified wife and children watched. And all for simply doing an honest days work which unfortunately for him was in a British court where honesty is deemed illegal.

Such brutal overkill would not be seen in front of witnesses for many years until MI5 ordered another public execution this time of the innocent Brazilian Jean Charles de Menezes at Stockwell tube station.

LR went on to explain to me how during decades of war between the IRA and the British state only pawns were ever killed. He made it clear that he did not wish to demean the dead. He was simply making a military observation which proved that MI5 had agents at the very top levels of the IRA. Agents who had the power to veto operations.

In all those years they had got a soft target royal Lord Mountbatten who regularly sailed off the Irish coast. They had also hit an MP in London. Other than those they had targeted pawns all over the board. One attack in Brighton was real but that was carried out by the small group INLA not the IRA. You can never win if you waste all of your time efforts and resources on pawns. You must target the major pieces and ultimately go directly after the king if you want to win war chess.

The fact that the IRA never went near the hierarchy of their enemy, in other words their true enemy, that proves that they were being subverted and held back by MI5 agents. That fact must therefore lead you to the conclusion that most of the innocent victims of IRA atrocities were perceived as expendable by the British state who let the operations go ahead in order to hide the complicity of their agents and to justify seizing more human rights and creating a police state.

In Britain we all hated the IRA bombers. If you look just a bit deeper you will see that our rulers forced the opposition to take such desperate steps and often allowed the attacks to be carried out. Who is the worst?

Two years before my talk with LR the IRA had declared another ceasefire on the 31st August 1994. During the following negotiations Mi5 tried to scupper the peace deal by bullying disrespecting and making unreal demands.

The Irish had grown very wise and they realised now that the British economy was being shored up massively by the revenue that is generated by the bankers in London's Docklands. In February 1996 the IRA (to use a quote) 'bombed the arse out of Docklands' causing massive damage and vast monetary losses. As anticipated the bankers rounded on the government and told them to pull their socks up. Money doesn't just talk, it gives orders.

The rulers were at last forced to do the right thing. The threat of losing all of that money left them with no choice other than to begin proper peace talks. Just over one year later in July 1997 the IRA were persuaded to declare another ceasefire. Eventually a power sharing peace deal was signed on Friday April 10th 1998 and it became known as the Good Friday Agreement. The (then) Prime Minister Tony Bliar tried to claim the credit however he was no more than a postman.

Back in 1996 in Perth prison I was analysing and memorising as much of the story of the Irish struggle to date and I was amazed by some of the stories that LR told me. He talked too much and I could not understand why. Two events, years apart gave me the answer. One day LR was right in the middle of an AK47 spraying heavy gangster story and I was all ears when suddenly two other prisoners started fighting. It was a feeble effort with a couple of half hearted punches, they then fell to the floor for a cuddle contest, mugs. I looked back at LR eager to hear the rest of the story but his face was chalk white and he had lost track of his tale. I stared closely at him for a long time in order to make sure that I was actually seeing straight, I was. He looked scared. I knew there and then that he was a grass. Piling up the bodies and the AK47's one minute then getting a fright when two dafties had a bogus roll about. LR was a coward and that was why he was so keen to impress with the war stories.

The next event came years later when LR was murdered in Glasgow. The media revealed that he had given evidence that secured the conviction of an alleged IRA hitman. LR had pretended to be a civilian witness but after his arrest for Loyalist gun running the alleged gunman got to appeal his sentence.

The lesson that I learned from that is even if you are looking into the eyes of a stone-cold paramilitary killer or into the eyes of the gangsterist gangster then you could still be looking at a spineless coward grass. You can never tell.

Today Ireland is becoming a great success story with a booming economy and plenty of new people bringing diversity into the country. The overall lesson there is that it is not healthy to be ruled by a foreign power especially if it happens to be the Windsors.

Ireland may you continue to grow forever more in tranquillity, prosperity and love. And may your dead sons and daughters all rest in peace.

That period of my life was all about lessons and some higher force seemed to be ensuring that I would not miss any. My arrest for robbing the jewellers in Perth had come about as a result of a number of chance events. 1. At the scene the traffic warden happened to be there and he got on his radio and gave a detailed description of our car and us. 2. A policeman happened to be only one street away arresting a shoplifter. He heard the radio call and jumped into his police car and immediately headed towards the jewellers. 3. Mr N's wild driving helped us to escape that police car. 4. The turf truck and the big lorry just happened to be blocking that road on our escape route at that exact time. 5. After we escaped again the police car at the top of the road just happened to round the corner and the passenger looked up in our direction at the exact moment that we had cleared the trees and were stepping onto the open path.

When life clicks into place in such a manner, and mine always does in both positive and negative events, then it is wise to

open up to every energy and any potential lesson.
I have only mentioned some characters and events here. It would take ten books to pass on every lesson that I learned while I paid my debt for going oyster catching.

4 True Calling

The date came up for us to appear in court to answer for the jewellers job. Mr N and I were looking at a few years each. We had basically committed a strong shoplifting. His replica pistol and shouted threats at the shop workers made it a robbery however we had not hurt anyone and the 13 watches did not add up to that much value.

Incidentally one worth £10K had vanished. There is no question that a policeman stole it, my only surprise is that they managed to control themselves and just take one watch.

We were taken to Aberdeen sheriff court for the high court sitting. The judge was Lord Osborne. Both legal teams said that he was fair and decent. That was good and surprising news.

Most jurors believe that all defendants are guilty before even hearing any evidence. In Scotland you get a third off your sentence for a guilty plea. So please pay more attention if you are ever on a jury because there is often a very good reason why someone would risk getting a guilty verdict and a sentence one whole third longer. It is relatively rare but on occasion that reason is innocence.

We expected five years each for the crime. Lord Osborne gave us some grief about the robbery and in particular he made it very clear that he was not happy with us for not giving back the missing watch. Our route was traced and searched and nothing was found because a copper had stolen it. We had to take a kick in the nuts for his crime because there are no dishonest policemen.

The judge gave Mr N Six years then gave me Seven years. He did not appear to have any malice and did not seem to get any pleasure from it. A rare breed in that profession. Presumably he gave me one year more than Mr N because I had just finished that three year sentence and did not seem to have learned my lesson. Despite what he believed, I had learned lessons alright.

I took the sentence on the chin with no anger, we had given the people in the shop a bad fright so the punishment was just. Negative actions never bring positive rewards. Even when people get away with a crime they invite bad luck into their lives by creating negative waves of energy in the world.

You will never see a truly happy crook.

We were quickly returned to Perth prison and the local papers had a bit of a splash about our robbery. Some of the workers and the two policemen who had arrested us were all given medals and bravery awards. They were in photos holding up their medals beside a smiling Mayor. It was true that their actions had been selfless and brave and they were due commendations but it was an every day thing where we came from so we found the hype a bit amusing.

It is not wise to tackle robbers. Lucky for these guys we were kinder than the average. Hopefully none of the people were frightened too much and perhaps it has become an exciting and interesting story for them to tell their friends. My burden would be lighter if that was so.

Mr N immediately put in a request to be moved to Shotts maximum security prison in Lanarkshire. It was only a ten minute drive for his visitors whereas the trip to Perth was one hour each way.

Shotts has a terrible reputation and has had repeated riots and numerous screws have been stabbed up and had legs and backs broken and all sorts of madness. There was even a machete smuggled in a few years ago and people were lending it to their friends in each hall who would chop their enemies into some mess. Only recently the jail was completely locked up and every single cell was searched by teams of police with sniffer dogs looking for handguns.

I also put my name down for a move to Shotts. It would make the travelling time much easier for my visitors so it was the best thing to do despite the apparent danger.

Shotts is a modern prison. The halls are not like the huge Victorian buildings that you see in films. From outside it resembles council tenements with grey cladding but with strange metal roofs. Every hall consists of three levels. And each one is simply a long corridor. There are stairs and the screw's office in the middle of every floor and off to the sides there are rows of cells, about 18 in each section. The ceilings are low and the cells are all squashed together with two rows facing one another only two steps apart so when you come out of your cell door you are within touching distance of the cell next door and the two cells opposite yours.

At that time big metal gates were kept locked in order to

contain any disturbance to one section before it could spread into a full riot. The result was that the screws hardly ever ventured into the sections unless they had to. Also there were not hundreds of other prisoners running wild so you could actually relax a bit. Both elements together meant that there was none of the oppression that you get in the large halls favoured by the private sector, the Victorians and the Americans. Your space and your time was your own and therein is the opportunity for growth if you stay drug free. Only a minority of prisoners have the strength to stay sober, those who do can reap the benefits.

In a small section of cells you can keep to yourself and if you are not naughty then you don't have to fear your neighbours too much. When the screws stay back and don't act aggressive or snide then you can relax and be yourself. That allows you to reflect and analyse your own character.

A psychologist once made an interesting observation about man. His theory was that we all have a set of needs. First we have hunger, thirst and the need for sleep. Next comes safety from danger then shelter from the elements. Next is the need for belonging and the need for love and lastly the need for status and achievement. He believed that once all of those needs are met then we can strive towards personal fulfilment. At which point we can become what we are destined or are meant to be such as a painter or a musician or a poet and so on.

His theory is probably sound however in the modern world most of us fulfil our needs past hunger, thirst, sleep, security and shelter. We get thrown off when it comes to the need to belong and to love and be loved. We often get those two basic needs mixed in with the next two needs for status and achievement. The corporate machinery that feeds us it's propaganda from birth to death makes most of us think that back is front. We come to believe that if we can manage to earn enough money then that will let us buy plenty of goods (house cars jewellery designer clothes etc) then we can use these things to show our status and the more expensive they are the higher levels we will reach. And so our goods will make us so attractive that we will find love.

That is the distorted view of reality that most people come to hold. Such a confused mindset results in even more anguish and sadness when the majority of people never come close to fulfilling their needs. Because no matter how much you can earn there will always be someone making more and you get sucked into the stupidity of status chasing more and more until you can never get enough and never be happy.

You cant blame the corporations they are only trying to earn as much money as possible. It is not their fault that their slick advertising actually warps reality for most people.

Instead of goods perhaps we should be focused on personality that is something that cant be bought and can never be taken away. The things that you do and think are your true measurement.

We are being taught that wealth is more important than personality. Ruthless directors at the top of every corporation including the media benefit from such distortions. The route though is purely a natural result of advertising techniques and trends. The resulting rat race is the reason why the majority of mankind today are blindly chasing dreams and never have the time to settle and find their true self or their true calling. We are too busy enslaving ourselves to corporate myths.

Far away from such distractions many prisoners manage to look deep inside and realise their potential. In jail it has been proven that complete solitary confinement damages the minds of the victims. Equally, overcrowded prisons like Barlinnie Perth and Saughton have too many prisoners doing too many things and not enough staff to keep watch never mind take an interest. Added to that is the brutality and the drugs epidemic. Such places have also been proven to damage the minds of the victims.

Shotts jail strikes something of a balance. The halls are small, contained and quiet (noisy neighbours get battered into silence, an asbo from a psycho). The screws back then did not interfere with every day life unless they absolutely had no other choice so there was no air of oppression or aggression or fear.

On a personal level I managed to grow in Shotts. A significant amount of my fellow prisoners did the same and all enjoyed the opportunity to relax, reflect and look within ourselves in order to find our true purpose. There was a constant flow of beautiful paintings, enjoyable poetry and mountains of short stories and novels, predominantly works of fiction.

Most human beings have hidden talents that they never get to tap into. We should all try to settle and search for the goodness.

I had realised that I could write half decent short stories while in Barlinnie and now that I was in Shotts in a better environment I was settled emotionally and could tap right into the source. My Yoga practice was still helping in every way and during periods of meditation I would seek and soar throughout the universe in an attempt to find the answers to my unending questions.

By analysing my own character and abilities I could understand why I had always felt the need to help anyone who is being picked on. I do not fear the enemies no matter how many or how strong, I normally always try to steam in. I am not a master storyteller however writing is communication, no more no less and I'm sure that most people can follow my words.

Most of my pals in jail (like me) came from the west of Scotland and have no real school education. The west coast is a violent place and Glasgow in particular is the murder capital of Western Europe. The people are not bad we are simply suffering from a combination of factors. First and most damaging is poverty, it is widespread. Most families are so busy working hard trying to survive that they have to leave much of their children's education in the hands of the schools, many of which provide a very poor service. Judging by the curriculum and the end results, most schools are aiming at best to create dull and placid manual labourers.

Many parents only find the time to ask their children a few questions and to dispense some quick advice like, 'try hard at school and look after yourself, don't let anyone pick on you and don't cause any trouble'. Better parental feedback is essential and unfortunately that fact is not known in much of Scotland.

The questionable school curriculum is a major factor in the violence. Our schools teach religious education which I personally believe is a waste of time because it is often full of lies and is severely hampered by its age and irrelevance. Spirituality cannot be forced.

They also teach a false history with undiluted propaganda about our alleged loving and caring rulers. The brain washing is so powerful that today you could do a word association test on anyone who has suffered this education system.

Take the words 'Princess' or 'Prince' and the response associated words every time will all be positive. Yet look at any real life princess or prince from true history and you will see a negative character.

Take princess Elizabeth who had her own cousin Mary Queen of Scots put through a bogus trial in order to murder her and continue with the theft of the country for herself. And even if Mary was the guilty one, she had also been a princess and she stood accused of plotting to murder her cousin Elizabeth to steal the country from her.

Look at the Spanish Prince Peter (the cruel) who murdered many people including his closest relatives. Look at prince Vlad Dracul nicknamed The Impaler because he would slaughter innocents by impaling them onto large stakes. He surrounded his castle with thousands of impaled men women and children and would eat his food and dip his bread in bowls full of children's blood. They are all ancestors of the Windsors who rule over us today.

The media is not some omnipotent benevolent being. Altogether it is simply a group of corporations who are there to make money not to help anyone or to bring the truth. When you have power money or information the media is there for you to use in whatever way you please and they will literally print anything that you want. The result is that the current royals have almost absolute control over the media so we don't get to see a true picture of their personalities. They play us a cartoon version of reality. However as the saying goes 'the apple does not fall far from the tree' meaning that many character traits are inherited and if we measure the royals by their ancestors then the true picture is terrifying.

The propaganda that is force fed to our children is designed to bolster the myth of the royal, religious and justice systems as all being good when in actual fact you only need to take a slightly closer look and you will see that they are not as they seem hence their need for the barrage of false history lessons.

Perhaps our schools should be teaching our children things that are relevant to their modern environment. First and most important is communication skills. The main reason why teenagers are involved in more violence than their elders is because many cannot properly communicate. Next is problem solving teaching it should be no problem. After that is the Thatcherite ethic of 'fuck you all I'm doing well'. Surely children could be steered away from such weakness and taught with a more sensible and progressive curriculum. There is also the problem of the corporate machine. It literally cuts the people away from the planet. Kids can easily identify hundreds of corporate logos but they have no idea about ecology. The world and everything in it is perceived as property to be used and exploited by corporations. That lets the people deny responsibility for the environment, it is left up to others to fix problems.

Perhaps every school should be funded to provide free uniforms and all logos should be discouraged. The teachers could then concentrate on attempting to mould the pupils into decent characters instead of the current practice of letting big business take control and create label and wealth obsessed insatiable consumers. Basic elements if taught to our kids would literally eradicate at least half of the violence.

The adults who have been denied these essentials often fall foul of the law. Ignore the weak bullies for now and look at strong men who happen to commit acts of violence. Many are above average intelligence yet are below average with regards to any educational qualifications. They were intelligent enough to see through the dark hood to the truth and thereafter switched off to the school system. Such wasted potential creates a need and with that comes frustration. Their struggle to get up out of poverty often tempts them to get involved in criminality. Their suffering can cause empathy and with that often comes anger at injustice.

When such a man commits an act of violence it is the result of him policing his own immediate environment. He cant go and attack the worst offenders like Bush or Blair no matter how many war crimes or smarmy smiles they show in the aftermath. However he can and will stop people who misbehave to a serious level within his presence or that of his nearest and dearest. When you see some fighting you are often looking at the end result of a poor education mixed with higher than average intelligence mixed with suffering and frustration and anger. That same man could live to 100 and never have so much as one fight in his life. He will only react to nasty situations not cause them. I have recognised some of those traits and behavioural patterns in myself and in every otherwise good man who I have met in prison.

It is in the interests of the establishment to see such guys wasting their lives away on the low level wrong yins on the streets rather than wake up and look up and decide to target the higher levels such as the aforementioned Bush and Blair. Again surely children could be educated properly. It is a statistical fact in Scotland that most people who are victims of knife crime will amazingly suffer another knife attack within the next year. The media and the courts perpetuate the carnage by ignoring the real issues and by using their stories of the violence to frighten and manipulate the masses. They declare every single fight as an unprovoked attack – 'unprovoked means that it could happen to you so buy this newspaper or watch this news channel to learn more. And be happy that we spend so much of your tax money on the criminal justice budget in order to protect you from the violent maniacs'. Please ignore such lies.

The reality is that most fights happen in and around pubs and clubs at night. Alcohol lowers inhibitions so bullies feel free to misbehave. Whether they are woman beaters or trouble makers who pick on the weak or are just general all round assholes, drunkenness makes them believe that they can act in any way.

Bullies have the small dog syndrome. If you walk past a large Pit bull it knows that you are no threat. As long as you don't mess with it then it wont pay much attention to you. When you walk past a small dog it panics and barks in a feeble attempt to scare you off. Bullies have that same problem which makes them panic and act loud and aggressive. They are trying to scare everyone away and they will quickly resort to violence against weaker people like smaller men or wives or girlfriends. What they never seem to learn is that loud aggressive behaviour against weaker people is the very thing that will draw strong men in and get them into some serious trouble.

All of what I had learned above gave me the inspiration to put my writing to good use and in Shotts I wrote a short story 'The Beast' where a group of men frustrated at the twisted legal system teach a lesson to a rapist.

The guys in Shotts loved it and some raved about it for weeks. The greatest success was that some privately declared a hatred for me. Clearly they could see their own characteristics in those of the fiend and they imagined me as one of the punishers.

Next I aimed higher. I exposed the worst people in our society and history, I realised that the tyranny can only continue if the people remain asleep. My work then was intended to wake the readers up.

It was obvious that I would also be alerting the true enemy but I do not fear them. In fact their history and behaviour makes me so angry I happily accept the danger.

Perhaps they realised that because ultimately they did make a move on me and I will cover it in chapter Seven. The reason why I have mentioned the stories that I wrote in Shotts is because they had a massive and unforeseen effect on my life. They were not the route of what was to come but they were definitely a factor.

Further studies in Shotts brought me more disturbing truths which I wrote down and (some would now say) I foolishly made a large number of copies and gave them out to my fellow prisoners. I asked them to read the stories and if they were enjoyable then they should send them out to their families and ask those people to read and pass them on. I would love it if you did that with this book. Knowledge is power and the spreading of it is essential for the survival of good people who are trapped under the boot of tyranny.

I wanted solid guys to see the game for what it is and to use that new knowledge to make better choices in future. Just a small piece of knowledge can change the entire course of someone's life. Therefore the more information, the greater the potential for positive change.

However I did not realise just what sort of monster I had awakened with my reckless behaviour. In hindsight I should never have revealed myself as a threat to the lies of the system with only a small amount of words and with such a small readership. One good thing is that they must now wish that they had killed me rather than what they eventually did. They have made a mistake in leaving me alive to do this work. This book will last far into the future. You cant kill truth.

My best short story was 'The Other Tribe'. I did a quick version and only gave it to a close group of good soldiers. It had such a powerful effect that I did a long one and put it out wide to as many readers as possible. The following chapter gives you a look at an updated version of part of it. You will be taken back in time and have your eyes opened to reality.

As always, don't just take my word for any of this. Make your own enquiries and come to your own conclusions. I want good souls among you readers to wake up, to pay attention and then investigate for yourself. Ultimately it is in your interest to understand the true dangers. Add to Darwin, this is survival of the most knowledgeable.

5 The Other Tribe

I don't have a crystal ball but I am very inquisitive and have a great hunger for knowledge and when I analyse properly I can come up with a history lesson that is closer to the truth than the nonsense that is force-fed to us all by those who have a reason to lie. You don't have to take my word for it, you are welcome to do your own research and come to your own conclusions. What you must do is try to understand the nature and the true history of our rulers and our system, what it has become today and where it is going. In my opinion we are rushing blindly towards disaster in Britain and it is our duty to attempt to avert the coming catastrophe. I beg you therefore to look for yourself, analyse rationally, learn as much as you can and then teach in order that as many people as possible learn enough to wake up and attempt to save themselves.

The biggest threat to the thief kings of old were the innocent masses who were the true owners of the country. The kings could no longer rely on blatant mass murder and had to attempt to control the people with fake religion and it's genocide. Next they used one on one murder which they gave a false stamp of legitimacy by way of the specially created justice system.

The warlords of old who had maintained control on behalf of the kings all had dungeons beneath their castles and forts. They would hold suspected criminals in the cells while they investigated the crimes and eventually they would kill the victims using various methods. Such injustice and fake authority began to cause dissent so the king changed the warlords title to Law Lord and had special courts constructed all over the land. The courts were allegedly owned by the people. They were no longer inside the warlord's castle so he could now sit in judgement and pretend to be independent of the court and would actually claim to be representing the people who believed they owned those courts.

Such things as trivial as eating a rabbit was still a crime according to the mafia and you would suffer a show trial and still be declared guilty and would be murdered at the end.

In the minds of the monarchs you were a threat if you did

not show absolute servitude to their system. If you were starving to death then you had to fear the mob so much that you would die rather than break the rules and eat any of the king's property.

If you broke the law then you were questioning the rulers by your actions and for such a heinous crime you had to die. Even worse was to speak the truth about the authority of the rulers. If you could see that anything was wrong with the system then you would be killed.

They would not simply murder their victims but would subject them to all kinds of perverted torture before death. When questions were raised about such disgusting acts they simply called it a trial by torture which was allegedly in an attempt to determine the truth and to find any accomplices.

The administrators of justice soon learned that murdering everyone who fell into their clutches was not a deterrent against other 'criminals'. A great many people were refusing to starve to death and were actually stealing food. They had to be stopped.

It was decided to hold the punishment part of the sentence in public. Crowds would be invited to gatherings where so called criminals would be slaughtered in front of your very eyes in order to warn you not to mess with your superiors.

Many forms of torture were used from the Rack to being boiled alive to pouring molten lead through your eyes. Hundreds of methods were tried out until the punishment of Hung Drawn and Quartered was adopted as the universal technique. You would be battered mercilessly then hung by the neck until you came close to unconsciousness, next you would be brought down tied to a table sliced open and have some of your intestines cut and torn out then thrown onto a fire in front of you. Next they would attack the genitals, the breasts of women and the penises of men would be sliced off and thrown in the fire.

When you were on the brink of death a mad Axeman would hack off your arms and legs and throw them onto the fire before finally chopping off your head. And yes you would suffer those horrors for even the most minor crime because all criminality was viewed as anti authority. Naturally it did not take long for public distaste to explode until eventually the law perverts had to content themselves with 'just' hanging you to death.

Tens of thousands of alleged law breakers were hanged in public and yet the people still refused to starve under the tyrannical regime. They still had the audacity to break the kings laws. A Bill was written up which listed two hundred crimes for which you would be hanged. That system was and always has been a power struggle. It identifies and destroys anyone who is not weak enough to capitulate to the rulers. Whether your crime involves you stealing food or money for survival or using physical means to protect yourself or others you are letting the man see that you are not a sheep. That makes you a potential threat to the system.

They will take your life away in front of everyone else in the hope that any other strong independent people will be scared off. The establishment have that same small dog syndrome, it fills them with fear and makes them panic and lash out ferociously.

At the heart of ordinary acts of theft and violence though are factors that will never be understood by such demented cowards. You have already seen the route causes of much violence. The other major crime is theft. Discard the manufactured problem of drug dependency and theft is predominantly a result of varying degrees of poverty. You can never erase poverty or theft, our Russian friends took a while to discover those facts.

We no longer have able bodied people starving to death in Britain so I will concentrate on thieves who work for gain. Every crook is a gambler at heart and when you mix that gambling spirit with need then you have a recipe for theft. Even when there were two hundred different crimes that would get you hanged you still had starving people stealing of course yet there also were robbers such as Dick Turpin and the like.

All crooks are driven by their needs or perceived needs and by their gambling spirit. No one in the history of crime has ever gone to work expecting to be caught. All criminals are just like the fools who make the bookmakers and the casino owners rich, they all believe that this time they will get a good result.

The establishment could murder the entire family and the next crook would still try because he never believes that he will be caught.   They could fit everyone up and have a one hundred percent detection and conviction rate and the gambling spirit would still convince him that he will be the one that gets away.

Walk into any betting shop and you will see a crowd of sad faces mostly all losers yet watch the very next one who walks through the door and he will happily join them and throw his hard earned money away over the counter absolutely certain that he will be the one who wins.   That gambling spirit is a form of mental illness in one sense yet it is also what gave our ancestors the courage to leave the caves and fight for control over the elements and the wild animals.

Our species would not have survived if it were not for the slightly mad people who thought that they could fight the lions and tigers and bears and ultimately to survive all threats while travelling over the world at their leisure.   Picture a wee five foot tall caveman who stumbles upon a large aggressive hungry bear.   He thinks to himself, 'If I can just kill that big bastard it will feed my family for a moon and if I skin it then I can make a good warm coat for my wife.   In fact if this dash ends in a good result here then I'm sure to get a blowjob tonight'.

That is who you were and essentially it is who you still are. So even if the authorities did have an absolute detection and conviction rate and even if they did slaughter the entire family of any criminals there would still be no dent put in the trends concerning provoked violence or crimes for gain as a result of need. The solutions are proper education to tackle violence. To tackle need requires compulsory buy back of all state assets, cancelling all PFI contracts (they were signed by gangsters like Tony Bliar and Jack McConnell so they are null and void) greater social spending, proper and stringent regulation of corporations and greater rights for workers.

As already stated after public torturing and butchering went out of fashion the establishment were stuck with the relatively quick murder by hanging.   One day there was a revelation. Italians (as sneaky as their man Machiavelli) had built arenas where they would divert the people's attention away from the tyrannical political system.   Gladiators would fight to the death to keep the masses focused on a few stupid fights while the real fight for control over the country went on quietly in the corridors of power. See football and celebrity watching for the modern equivalent.

Just like the British, the Italians also murdered all criminals and undesirables. They would not hang them though, they would arm them and throw them into the arenas where the gladiators would make sport before eventually slaughtering the victims.

During a time of political embarrassment a mass killing was ordered up as the usual diversionary tactic. A Centurion was given the task of rounding up enough victims for the show. If he could not make the numbers then he was assured that he and his men would do. Not surprisingly he managed to find enough criminals and the show was a success for the rulers.

After suffering immense pressure from having been forced to fit up so many innocent people and almost falling prey himself, the Centurion ordered some chambers to be cleared underneath the arena and for them to be used for stockpiling future victims. They would be fed and watered with the barest minimum required to keep them alive long enough during the stockpiling period. The captives were all locked inside one large room and their dates of entry were noted in order to kill them on the basis of first in, first out. Initially there was heavy violence and resistance when the names were called out and the damned would even try to steal the identities of their most recent neighbours in an attempt to avoid death. Eventually there was a lull in the political intrigue and the detainees were growing in number and spending longer in the dungeon due to lack of demand from the politicians.

After a period of some weeks there was again the need for mass killing and when the soldiers went to call out the names of those who were due to be sacrificed they were met with ferocious violence but the people were now fighting to be picked. They wanted to die!

The soldiers reported this strange phenomenon to the Centurion and when he watched the vicious fights for himself he immediately realised that in his dungeon he had inadvertently discovered a fate worse than death. Thus imprisonment was born.

It would be another few centuries before it spread fully. Today it is the modern version of public hanging and it is so effective that it is used all over the world. These days only religious fanatics like the Arab rulers and their pals the American rulers continue to execute people. Evil words sneaked into old books used to justify murder.

Many behaviourist psychologist inspired regimes and experiments have been used on prisoners in Britain. It has gone from mass imprisonment like that Italian dungeon, to solitary confinement to slave labour to forced non-productive labour and all of the way up to today where jails are no more than warehouses exactly like the overcrowded chicken sheds that you see campaigners shouting about.

Most jails have governors who order or allow the screws to bully brutalise and torture inmates. Barlinnie and Saughton are bad jails Kilmarnock is heading the same way and Glenochil now has the worst reputation for having the most perverted screws in Scotland. It is so entrenched in Glenochil that you would have to sack the entire staff and start again if you ever wanted to stop the abuse. Many members of the public have literally been murdered by ex-convicts driven into an uncontrollable rage by the tortures inflicted in Glenochil and Barlinnie.

It is crazy to allow the SPS to continue with their sick culture. The screws often take great pleasure in torturing people as an alleged crime prevention tactic however the governors must be wise enough to see that it is extremely damaging and creates future victims by warping prisoner's minds. Being forcibly snatched out of society and kept away is punishment enough. The time is meant to be used positively in an attempt to spark rehabilitation but that is smashed by governors and screws who take it upon themselves to add to the punishment with brutal and unjust treatment. It guarantees the jobs and pensions so perhaps that is their motive for allowing it to continue.

Please understand though, no matter what jail you are sent to it is indeed in many ways a fate worse than death. The only good point is that most of you are alive at the end of it. Consider how frustrated you get when you have to wait ten minutes for a bus or when you get stuck in a traffic jam for fifteen minutes or when you have to waste twenty minutes on the phone to a robot in a call centre or when you have to wait thirty minutes at the doctors.

Now imagine your frustration at being kept waiting in a less accommodating environment such as a stinking jail where the robots don't just fail to understand you and fail to address your needs but they actually make an effort to treat you like an animal and they often behave like beasts and batter and brutalise and torture you physically and psychologically. They can literally murder you and put it down as a suicide and they are not slow in making you very aware of the danger. Ninety-six percent of your fellow prisoners smoke so every breath that you take is full of cancerous poison that has already been inside the disease ridden lungs of your desperate addict neighbours. The multitude of negative emotions fill the jails until they all have sick building syndrome where you only have to step inside and immediately you feel sad angry and exhausted. It is illegal for you to earn money so your loved ones often suffer extreme deprivations on top of the agony at your absence and witnessing your torture. You have absolutely no control over anything whatsoever. You are given junk food every day that has been prepared by unclean drug addicts. Your entire life is in the hands of often spineless and vindictive people who are just as twisted as the insane system that employs them. Every day is filled with sickness and sadness and extreme stress and danger and frustration and anger and sensory deprivation and none of it ever stops. Tomorrow will be just as bad as yesterday and today. If you don't catch any diseases from the junkies in the cookhouse and if you somehow manage to avoid catching cancer from the constant clouds of smoke and if none of the resident psychos decides to kill you then one day the disturbed shadow of your former self will be set free.

How frustrated would you feel after ten minutes of that horror? What about ten whole days? Months? Years? Please believe me, prison is an extreme form of torture that does damage the mind of every single one of its victims to varying degrees.

It is absolute hell even for the prisoner who spends just three days locked up over an unpaid fine. Imprisonment is agony and is designed to be. The establishment have never been dragged too far away from their torture techniques of the past. They have simply moved on to psychological and mostly non-life threatening physical torture rather than the fatal physical versions. They are very clever when it comes to hiding the truth. The media make money for propaganda and they get most of their stories from the man: ministers, judges, prosecutors, prison screws and mostly from police. Inevitably the media become a mouthpiece for them.

Newspapers continually rattle on about 'soft' sentences and 'cushy' jails and all sorts of other lies that are designed to brainwash the public into believing that most people in the dock are guilty and jails are so cushy that even a life sentence is easy time so why not come back with a guilty verdict just in case the accused is guilty. As previously stated the Hollywood spinners do the same. The establishment don't want you to realise the true horrors of imprisonment because they rely on you to keep their crooked system working perfectly when you view the accused with a cynical eye and don't give them the benefit of the doubt and you don't feel that you are doing them much harm with a guilty verdict.

Tony Blair was asked if he would ever bring back hanging. He said that he would LOVE to however he could not because jurors would take the case more seriously and would pay too much attention to the [lack of] evidence and would only come back with a guilty verdict if they were absolutely convinced of the defendants guilt so conviction rates for murder would drop and that is why he could not bring back capital punishment.

The reporter was stunned to hear such an inhuman answer and said, "I thought you were going to say that there have been too many miscarriages of justice in Britain and you would not want to kill any more innocent people."

Blair's eyes glazed over and he said, "I would rather see one innocent person go to prison for life than see nine guilty people walk free.'

He would never be so evil if it was his son who happened to be one of the innocent people locked up for life. And it is not true that a legitimate and fair legal system would result in guilty people walking free. That is a myth created by lazy inhuman state appointed criminals who are happy with the system which provides high wages in easy jobs at the destruction of genuine justice.

It is of course easy for Bliar to have such perverted ideas because the law and the courts in Britain are weapons of war that are used by the ruling elite to keep control and ownership of the stolen country.

When the media tell you that jails are soft and that sentences are too short they are perpetuating a lie on behalf of their hidden masters. The front line of people who suffer most from such lies are not prisoners, it is the victims of crime who are hurt further and especially the families who have lost a loved one. They scream that sentences are too short and they imagine that jail time is easy and that life should mean life. Believe me ten years in prison is enough brutal torture to completely erase any life that was ever in anyone.

Jail kills you from the inside out and there is no escape from the agony. Any more than ten years of uninterrupted imprisonment is merely dressing for the public. All of these 11 years and upwards minimum recommendations are purely to make propaganda headlines.

They are a massive waste of time and taxpayers money because after ten years you are flogging a dead horse. The person who was there is long dead and only an empty carcass remains. There are rare events with killers re-offending but the majority of lifers when they eventually do get out shuffle off and are never heard of again. That has always been true even back in the seventies and early eighties when the average lifer was released in under ten years.

It costs a minimum £40,000 per year to keep each prisoner in jail and some lifers are doing five, ten and even fifteen years on top of the man-eater ten years. Up to £600,000 of taxpayers money wasted flogging each one already dead prisoner just so politicians can secure headlines in newspapers and pretend that long sentences are good for anything. You only have to look at America to see they don't work.

Prisoners like Ian Huntly require to be incarcerated indefinitely. I do believe that we should lock up forever all sex offenders because they are incurable insane maniacs.

Yet most life prisoners in Scotland have had a knife fight. They did not want to kill or die and after ten years in jail they are just as dead as the victim, only a zombie version of them remains. It is a further crime against bereaved families to deny them that knowledge.

Some people even argue to bring back hanging. Firstly our legal system is completely top to bottom corrupt and is unsafe. Second and just as infuriating is when the idiots who want capital punishment argue that you should die if you take a life.

A man was stabbed seventeen times and managed to wrestle the knife from his attacker. He stabbed him once and the attacker died. The man survived. He had defended his life against a determined adversary yet he was sentenced to life for murder. If the moronic eye for an eye law was in place then the loonies would hang that man. What if that man's people also believe in the same eye for an eye madness and decide to kill the judge or the hangman for murdering him. Then the loonies call for them to be killed and on and on it goes until one day everyone is dead.

When you observe people you get an idea of what they are about. What is true for any individual is also true for any organised group. They can be watched, assessed and you should be able to get a measurement of the character of the average member.

Consider a group of football hooligans. You can look at their behaviour and easily work them out. Or take a group of environmentalists you can quickly understand what makes them tick.

Now look at Sheriffs (or Magistrates) and Judges. I believe that you would have to be ill to want such a job in the first place given that it involves you having to follow sentencing guidelines and suspending your own humanity. You cant feel anything for the single mother who has stolen some food for her hungry kids, you have to protect big business and the economy from shoplifters so she must be sent to jail and her children taken away to a home. Surely only a weirdo would ever want or would take such a job that requires a suspension of all humanity.

My real point is that when you look at sentencing trends in our courts you can accurately work out what the rulers and their judges are truly about. You can see the nature of the beast when you survey its deeds. The information is there for you just pay attention.

Take the great train robbers as an example. They stole pieces of paper. They did give one man a knock on the head and the job did earn them a large sum of money. Essentially though all that they really did was steal some pieces of paper. Yet the establishment sentenced them to thirty years. One judge later voiced his alarm at the fact that the leader of the robbers had planned to send his son to private school. Granted the crime was wrong but who could see a father trying to give his son a better life as a bad thing.

The alarm and hatred towards the robbers exists to this day as the current members of the establishment have tortured poor old Ronnie Biggs. What they did to him and his son is disgusting and sickening and the media have been largely silent. The persecution is evil and it shows you how the legal system is still absolutely determined to stop anyone from taking shortcuts to wealth. Once they stole everything they pulled the ladder up after them and will stamp on the face of anyone who tries to follow. It all stems from the fear about the poor people having the courage to stand up and take back from the king what he had stolen from them. Organised theft therefore is a high priority crime for the man to clamp down with outrageous sentences.

If someone robs a bank for a couple of grand then ultimately he has caused a nuisance to an insurance company. Somewhere they will simply scam the money back from their customers as they do with every loss, they are the worst villains in the piece. So other than a bank employee getting a fright and the robbery causing some inconvenience there is no real damage done. Yet the courts will sentence the robber to at least five years and depending on his previous conduct that can go up to ten or even fifteen years. He has done wrong of course but there are levels.

Now consider a low life who snatches a bag from a pensioner. That crime causes a terrible fright to the degree where the victim may be too scared to ever get back to normal life. Also the money that has been stolen is not insured and is therefore irreplaceable. Yet the system constantly sentences these muggers to only a few months imprisonment. What does that tell you?

Scum who rob people in their homes of goods and life savings only get a couple of years. Yet burglars who break into commercial premises get at least four years. That tells you that the courts view money and rich corporations as more important than the decent individuals who truly need the courts protection.

People who batter women get lenient sentences in comparison

to men who fight equally strong and capable men. Fiends who murder their wives in unprovoked attacks get at least five years less than those who kill their wives during a fight and the discrepancy is even greater between the first group and men who kill other men in a fight. What does that tell you?

Individuals who carry out unprovoked attacks upon the vulnerable are perverted and our rulers perhaps see them as kindred spirits. In contrast, men who fight equally strong adversaries may one day try to fight the establishment therefore they are perceived as a greater threat and are sentenced disproportionately. That trend alone must show you that the system is there to protect the establishment not the people. You pay for all of it yet it is abused and used predominantly for their protection, not yours.

By far the most informative and the sickest trend that is repeated in our courts the length and breadth of Britain is the sentences that are given to sex offenders especially paedophiles. Rapists get less than low level fraudsters and paedophiles get less than shoplifters. The rulers think very carefully about these sentencing guidelines.

People who feel the urge to force themselves on victims in sex attacks are not criminals, they are insane. And anyone who even remotely confuses children with potential sex must be completely and utterly crazy.

We can all understand a desperate illegal activity for monetary gain or an angry or fear filled act of violence, those are criminal acts. However there is no logical or sensible reasoning inside the mind of a sex offender, those are acts of madness.

Yet rather than protect society by rounding up all sex offenders and locking them up in asylums forever where they can do no more harm, the establishment instead treat them like friends and are very lenient with the sentences which are no more than tokens. And that is on the extremely rare occasions when the prosecutors have not ditched the charges and have actually taken the case to court. What does all of that tell you?

Think about it. We humans are sensitive creatures and don't like to be hurt, most of us can still feel the pain from some time in the past when someone upset us and hurt our feelings. We cannot even begin to imagine the life destroying agony that must be suffered by victims of sex attacks. After murder it is the most damage that anyone can do to another person. The absolute worst experience must be that which is suffered by children who are subject to such sickening behaviour. Sex attacks are unquestionably the second most serious crime on earth so why do our judges and our justice system view it and treat it as less serious than shoplifting?

Most shoplifters get at least six months. Most paedophiles get their charges dropped or get a fine or probation or just a couple of months imprisonment. What does that say about our judges and our system?

Put yourself in the judge's seat, what would you do? Personally I would look after kindred spirits. I would help men like me whether they had committed a robbery or simply had a fight, I do not view such actions in black and white terms and if offenders had mitigating circumstances then I would help them. That is only natural.

If you were a judge and you were asked to give someone a jail sentence for driving their car one day after the insurance policy has expired then you could not follow that sentencing guideline, your human nature would make you treat them leniently because you do not believe that people should be sent to jail in orders from insurance corporations who bung corrupt politicians to pressure police and the courts to attack all drivers no matter how small their indiscretion. You would help the driver because you are a human being and cannot act like a robot.

So now try to understand why every single judge in this country is happy to follow sick guidelines and help rapists and paedophiles with lenient sentences. What the hell is going on?

The media help them further because they very rarely ever tell the public how much time sex offenders are getting. They print the horrific stories but 99 times out of 100 they say that the rat will be sentenced at a later date. And when that date comes they never get round to telling you the length of the sentence because they have been asked to assist the judges in hiding the truth from you.

The public deserve to be protected from sex offenders. Judges who help sex offenders are in my opinion just as perverted and insane as them because their bogus sentences show that they do not believe that sex attacks are a bad thing. There is no other logical reasoning that can explain the behaviour of our law lords.

They are hiding the token sentences even deeper now by giving sex offenders public protection life sentences. The monsters still only do a year or two or a few months just as they always have done. Make your own enquiries and see for yourself how quick sex fiends get back onto the streets to prey again thanks to our deranged legal system.

Another informative sentencing trend relates to gun crime. I personally view guns as a cowards way to make himself an instant danger. They are unsporting and if you are not being shot at then you are cheating when you shoot unarmed people.

There is a massive discrepancy in gun-crime sentences. Two men were involved in some criminal activities and they went to shoot a rival, the victim survived and the gunman was sentenced to twenty years. His pal who had not even fired the gun was also buried alive with a twenty year sentence. They will have to serve a minimum ten years and that will go up to fifteen years if they don't get any parole time off.

Recently a sick beast threatened to murder an innocent woman when he argued with her husband. The freak kept the promise and broke into her house and brutally stabbed her ten times and when her young nine year old son tried to protect his mother, the bastard even stabbed the wee boy. In my opinion that monster is insane and should be locked up in an asylum indefinitely. Yet the judge only gave him eight years. That is less than half what they gave to the gunmen. He will have to do only between four and six years and like every other unsuitable prisoner he will be sent to an open prison while only a few genuine people share it with him and many suitable prisoners never get to see the place and he will be granted parole while many decent people are refused. And the establishment literally hope that when he gets out and attacks further innocent women and children they can use his case to scream in the media about soft jails and short sentences and will demand an end to parole. What does that tell you about our judges and our legal system?

Criminals have generally had good results from doing bad things and the parole system teaches them that they can get better results from good behaviour. It is clever manipulation and is one of the progressive things about the machine. That is why the people who's jobs rely on crime want to end parole because it does too much good. They try to end it by keeping life prisoners in past their tariff with no good reason in an attempt to enrage them and destroy any good that they have achieved internally and by giving unsuitable people like the aforementioned beast parole in the hope that he will go on another rampage and let them shout about ending time off for good behaviour. It is all a game to the maniacs who are running our legal system.

When someone is convicted of committing a murder with a knife they are sentenced to life with a minimum term of an average of twelve years. When the murder weapon is a gun then the sentence leaps up to almost double with an average of twenty years. That is further evidence that the system is there to protect the rulers not the people. You could never manage to harm the royals or any leading politicians with a knife so you are viewed as less of a threat to them. You could harm them with a gun however and the sentences that they give for gun crime reflect their nervousness.

Some years ago a young man fired one shot at a distance from a handgun to frighten another man unfortunately the bullet hit and the victim died. The gunman was sentenced to life with a minimum twenty years. It was an accident yet he will do at least twenty years. There is no parole time off a minimum life tariff. The sentence is twenty years plus life. After twenty years he can apply for parole off the rest of the life term but freedom is not guaranteed. If it had been an accident with a knife then he would have got about eight years for culpable homicide. The use of a gun means that he has at least sixteen extra years to do and those years are not for any reason other than the establishment panicking and making sure that he never gets to turn his gun totting attention to them.

They have every reason to fear because they know their true history and also what is planned for the future and that knowledge makes them terrified in case the good people ever get wise to it and revolt.

We have our own parliament in Scotland and I believe that we should besiege the politicians and demand change away from the sick sentencing trends that are set by the deranged advisors of the royals.

There are now roughly eight thousand prisoners in Scotland's jails. More than two thirds are doing useless and detrimental sentences of twelve months or less. Those sentences are too harsh a punishment for the charges faced and the prison environments and regimes create further crimes when they damage the minds of the victims.

Therefore in the interests of the public and genuine justice all such sentences of twelve months or less should be changed to non-custodial community work. The time could also be used to educate any offenders where required. Incarceration at £40,000 per year for each prisoner is a massive theft of taxpayer's money.

There would now be about Six Thousand spaces in our overcrowded jails. That would save £240 Million per year. We would also be protected from the future crimes of those offenders who avoid being warped by the agonising experience of imprisonment.

There are three and a half thousand sex offenders prowling our streets every day in Scotland. Some on the register will be innocent, so guilty pleas or guilty verdicts for three or more crimes against three or more unrelated victims would be a good measurement of guilt. The guilty ones are dangerously insane and should be treated as such. The bastards could be rounded up and locked up indefinitely and it would not cost one extra penny if we have already emptied our jails of the six thousand prisoners who are doing useless sentences of twelve months or less. That one move would make Scotland the safest country in the world and if it sparked a trend in other countries then Mother Nature herself would smile with joy and relief. And we should not hide behind any sort of legal rights or justice patter. Our courts are completely corrupt and no one who goes through them enjoys equality or rights or justice. The courts already take the lives of innocents without any bother so they could just as easily be made to take the lives of the guilty sex offenders.

Protect the innocent women and children, lock up sex monsters in asylums where they belong before they can do any more damage. Their condition is incurable and their attacks are intolerable therefore indefinite incarceration in asylums is the only real deterrent.

In Britain we now have roughly ninety thousand people locked up in prison. We jail more people per head than any other European country yet our crime rates have always remained average. And they do not significantly fall as the jail population rises. The reason that the true statistics do not tally is the rewards for information programme which is the engine of the entire justice system machine. The police have tried to hide the truth by constantly fiddling the statistics and re-categorising crimes and putting them into different lists.

The rewards for information programme is by far the biggest con that the authorities have wedged into our system. Did you never wonder why that despite tens of thousands of drug related arrests per year and despite ever increasing shipments being captured there is rarely ever a full dry up of drugs on the streets.

Did you never wonder why a drug business that raises an estimated £8 Billion per year in Britain alone only ever results in the small fish being targeted. You have all seen the footage of the Darth Vader helmeted police battering doors in and screaming at the top of their voices no doubt terrifying the women and children inside. Eventually they bring out the bad man, the dreaded drug dealer. Do you not find it strange that you have only ever seen them smashing down the doors of dilapidated council houses. They only ever arrest the poor addicts who are only dealing to feed their habits.

The big boys are left alone because heroin is the cause of ninety percent of all crime in Britain. Therefore the £15 Billion in taxpayers money that is wasted on the criminal justice budget per year and the literally hundreds of thousands of spies, police, forensic scientists, forensic accountants, customs officers, court staff, prosecutors, defenders, judges, prisoner transportation staff, prison staff, social workers, drug workers, doctors, nurses, chemists, psychiatrists, think tanks, drugs 'experts' and 'justice' ministers who are all kept alive with that money depend entirely on the heroin problem continuing along in order to keep them all stealing that money from you and pretending that it is for your own good. They could stop it all tomorrow by giving heroin free on prescription.

A senior police officer once estimated that eighty percent

of all people arrested in Britain were persuaded to give information by police and about twenty percent of those are registered licensed informers. When you consider that there are hundreds of thousands of convicted criminals in Britain then you can get an idea of just how many people have been given a licence to commit crime. And they will either have their sentences reduced, have the charges dropped or if they are at the top of the informer tree then they will never even be arrested. The grasses commit ten times more crime than anyone they ever inform on. That guarantees the survival of the machine with the resulting steady and often rising crime rates and at the same time it provides patsy's who serve as the casualties of the pretend war on drugs. It is a massive con.

Ask yourself how it can be that Britain's hundreds of thousands strong criminal justice army with it's £15 Billion per year budget never go near the so called godfathers. Do you not find that a bit strange?

One example from Glasgow was the man nicknamed the Licensee. He was suspected of having ordered or carried out at least fifteen murders during a 30 year criminal career. He worked as a licensed informer and hardly spent a day in prison. Thirty years of state sanctioned serious crimes including massive importation and distribution of drugs. He would provide the police with patsy's who would be set up and lifed up for the murders that he was behind that way his police handlers did not have unsolved crimes on their books. Like all big players, the licensee would set up couriers every time to let the police maintain the fake war on drugs. He would give up five kilos in one shipment and bring in one hundred right behind it. He would treat it like a tax as all major grasses do.

The culture of rewards for information is an extremely serious crime against the people however it is impossible to stop. The employees who are meant to administer justice are only human and they will take the shortcut every time. Also most people who commit crimes are weak and it is clearly not very hard to turn them over.

As for you good souls there may come a day when you are locked in a tomb naked and destroyed with a heavy sentence. You may have no hope, no dreams, no future yet you will have something that cannot be taken or even tortured out of you. That thing is your internal strength and pride. If you ever go over to the evil side and get on your knees for your enemy and give information then you will be lost forever, an empty soul. However if you take the pressure, take the torture and stay absolutely strong and determined then you will win. Remember this is not about anyone who you could inform on, it does not matter if you love or hate them, it is all about you. If you give up then you are truly lost. They can torture you or lock you up forever or even kill you but they can never win against you and they will know it. Most importantly you will know. It is not about what anyone else thinks of you, it is absolutely about what you truly know inside, so they can do and say anything and your internal pride and strength will be more than enough to get you through any torture or situation.

If we had a just system then things may be viewed differently by some. While we have the most corrupt legal system in Europe then it remains a crime against humanity to inform on crooks and subject them to the vile attentions of the devils legions if you yourself are involved in criminality. Remember they cannot physically take your pride you have to be weak enough to give it over and if you do then you are crawling on the ground with the maggots. Stay strong people, keep your soul clean.

If straight people just pay a little bit of attention then you will see that the refusal to give heroin on prescription and the added massive programme of rewards for information system together actually Cause ninety percent of crime in Britain.

Every battered pensioner, burgled house, snatched handbag, every prostitute raped (they only have sex to pay for the drugs so all of you who use them is a low life rapist) every drug overdose, every drug dealer murdered and every other incalculable act from the catalogue of carnage, all of those literally millions of crimes committed each year in Britain are heroin related and are caused by the very people who pretend to be fighting against it but actually who guarantee their own jobs by perpetuating it.

I have looked into this. It costs just £50 for one kilo of raw opium in Afghanistan. That is turned into eight kilos of street heroin. Each of those contains 10,000 wraps of heroin costing £10 each. That means you can get the equivalent of 10,000 wraps in pill form out of every kilo so for your £50 investment you could make 80,000 pills.

For just a tiny amount of money you could give every addict in Britain two pills per day each the size of a £10 deal. You could deny completely the enormous theft of taxpayers millions that is the useless and disgusting methadone programme. You could also deny the heroin prescriptions in jail as a way to prevent re-offending. You would also have to absolutely deny the prescriptions to anyone who was not born in this country that would prevent every junkie in the world coming here for free smack.

Heroin gets most of the addicts so desperate that they batter their own grannies for a fiver so free gear on the streets and none in jail would remove their need to commit crime, would enable them to feed and provide for their children and would serve as an absolute incentive to avoid all criminality. It would also be virtually impossible for non-users to try the gear therefore it would eventually eradicate the heroin problem.

It is a very simple and cheap solution. The addicts are on the gear every day anyway even in jail and most of them never want to stop so all of the bogus help is a complete waste of time. Drug addiction is the ultimate selfish pursuit so only the self can beat it.

The problem with implementing such a sensible solution as heroin on prescription is that for the past forty years our criminal justice army has been fed watered and pensioned thanks to the fake war on drugs.

So until you demand it of your politicians with every voice raging in their ears then you will continue to suffer and continue to pay your £15 Billion in tax money and pay with £8 Billion in stolen money and goods and untold social carnage year after year after year while the people who can stop it continue to tell you lies cash your fat cheques and laugh up their well tailored sleeves.

Don't accept it. Don't ignore it. Don't just take my word for it. Do make your own enquiries and come to your own conclusions and then get yourselves into groups as large as possible and lay siege to your local MP and MSP. Do not stop hounding them until you create change. They allegedly work for you and they do receive your tax money so make them do your bidding. Change your world.

6   Blue Skies

I had found the uncomfortable answers to many questions and was determined to enlighten as many people as possible. I had no idea just what I was cooking up for my future by making the ill ones aware that I was onto them and was not scared and not too shy to tell anyone who would listen.

I spent my last year in Shotts prison full of hope and positive ideas for the future. I continued to read study and write stories around the truths that I discovered. I trained hard in the gym doing weights and was also spending one hour per day running. I had lots of positive responses to my stories, they woke up some good people and persuaded them to choose a wiser path. If I also managed to persuade some wrong yins to behave then great.

My parole hearing came up, I had now been locked up for three years six months. It had been a long hard journey however I had managed to stay reasonably sane and my determined effort to turn my life around and stop serving myself up as food for these people eventually paid off and I was granted parole.

I was so out of my mind with floods of amazing emotions that I could not honestly describe those last days in Shotts. I was floating. At last after so long I was going home and this time I would stay free forever.

I had suffered enough for one lifetime. It was now time for me to embrace a new life full of love and positive behaviour. No more adrenalin chasing. No more wild pursuits. No more jail.

I walked out of Shotts much fitter than I had ever been yet I was in some emotional pain from my years of incarceration and was also hurting a bit with the burden of some of my new found knowledge. I learned to place all of that pain inside a storage box in my mind. From now on it would be love all the way. Freedom at last.

I strolled into the best two years of my life. The first days were a blur of mixed emotions. Such a long period of incarceration with all of the problems that it holds like stress for 24 hours per day for the entire period and prolonged sensory deprivation damages the mind. It is very difficult to get over the experience and adjust to the new world which freedom delivers you into. Sensory overload causes a sort of drunkenness.

When you were a child and you ate too many Easter eggs you were amazed to find that chocolate, often the best food in your young world, can actually make you feel dizzy and sick. That is what freedom brings. The multitude of sights sounds smells flavours textures events and emotions are all too much for your brain to take on board. While everyone else has honed their senses in order to dull down background information, the sensory starved mind of the ex-convict has lost that ability and is driven half mad with the overload until everything blends into one. That blending must be an internal autonomous process designed to prevent meltdown.

Your social skills are also severely damaged after years of talking to only a small hand picked group of trustworthy friends and your common conversations have mostly all been concerning crime and punishment. Suddenly one morning you are in a room filled with normal people who are talking about the weather or holidays or the mortgage rate and you feel like an alien among your own family.   People who have loved and cared for you and brought you up are separated from you in unbearable ways. You pray that one day you will get back to normal and will again be connected to the rest of humanity and will be even remotely interested in life's little things.

You look at your people through a drunken haze and see their souls. It is amazing to come from an insanity inducing prison and suddenly find yourself in a room full of love and good souls. Soldiers who die on the battlefield must experience an extreme form of the same thing when they are suddenly snatched out of the hell of warfare and are delivered to their ancestors in the land of light and love on the other side.

I was very lucky with my trade as a tiler. I managed to get straight back to work and with every job I was tasting gentle amounts of the real world as I worked in each household meeting good people and bringing them happiness with my perfectionist work. As I met more people I was gradually coming back down to reality and working towards balancing my senses.

I joined my friends who were still partying most nights on the town and this time I stayed sober. They still had a couple of fights on occasion but I stayed out of it. That sort of thing was a Neanderthal version of me I was too far in front spiritually to go back there. If any of them were in danger of being badly hurt then I would have helped them but a thrill chasing battle across the streets no longer held any attractions for me.

One night I struck gold only days out of prison when I was introduced to a friend of a friend in a nightclub. I was not paying much attention when suddenly her voiced caressed my ears with beautiful words that make me smile to this day. "My boyfriend is a policeman."

Every punch and kick, every piece of bullshit evidence, every minute of my torture in the hellhole Barlinnie during that first jail term was about to be repaid with love. (I deserved the sentence in Perth and Shotts for the robbery so held no bitterness on that). After I had delivered the love to her, he would only be alerting her to his inadequacies whenever he tried in future. It could be that he was one of the decent few however the odds were on that he was one of the rats. She would get to sample the stark difference between me (a caveman) and him (a poof).

In bringing her to my attention the forces of goodness and light were on my side that night. I smiled and said to her, "well lets see who's the best the cops or the robbers." I took her hand and walked her out of the club and into the nearest taxi.

We went back to her house where I went straight to work and I put three and a half years of frustration into the job and I really gave her the benefit of all of that added on top of my fitness level from my constant training and running in the gym. I don't care who you put me up against, you could bring in Rambo and the 300 Spartans and together they would still not be able to equal the pleasure that I delivered that night. In the morning I asked her who was the best and she assured me that the title was won by the robbers! Good on you hen.

Life went on and I met new people, I don't want to reveal their identities or even any details or the circumstances surrounding any of our relationships and the reasons for that will become clear later on. I want to protect them as much as possible by not revealing anything. It must be said though that new friends were a blessing. I also remained close to all of my old friends of course.

Everything seemed to click into place for me whenever I needed it, my positive mindset was paying me back and all was well. I was into the teachings in the Celestine Prophesy books by James Redfield and I bought copies for a few people. I started trading used cars, a number of my friends are car dealers and I would buy some of their trade ins. Only the cheap ones at £1500 or less. I went into partnership with two other traders and did as much car selling as I could in between my ceramic tiling work.

My efforts to readjust into society were bringing positive effects slowly and surely. I was renting a tiny flat in the merchant city district of Glasgow however I spent much of my time at my new girlfriend's house. All previous tortures were slowly being forgotten.

Christmas was coming up and I was on the best job that I have done, it was a living room and hall floors in a terraced house in Glasgow. My dad came in to lay a latex level screed for me. The customers had picked beautiful cream tiles and my dad persuaded them to take a mosaic style thick border which he promised to design and lay like a rug in the middle of the living room floor. We also used a four-inch cutting as a ceramic skirting round the walls.

The family were friendly with my dad he had done some work for them in the past and he wanted me to really make a job of these floors. To top it all they bought an expensive cream stone fireplace which set the tiles off perfectly. It was a big job and my dad left me to it, only coming back for one day to lay the mosaic border design and sure enough it looked forever like a big rug. It was beautiful.

I carried on and got the living room floor finished, the hall had three doorways a cupboard and a set of stairs not to mention the front door, in other words plenty of work. I managed to run the line of tiles out of the living room perfectly and set about cutting into all the doorways. It was nearly Christmas and I was determined to have the job done and get out of their way so I did a twelve hour shift one day then a thirteen hour shift the next. The day after that I was finishing off grouting the hall when blood appeared on the tiles, I checked my hands for the cut. Just at that the customer appeared and told me that the blood was coming from my nose. I sorted it out and got back to work and she told me that I was working too hard, I had to agree. I am glad that I did that job though because I have done plenty over the years including bathrooms where the customers have spent thousands of pounds on the tiles alone and still that floor remains my favourite, it came out absolutely perfect. I took her advice on board and eased up a bit with my tiling work and tried to shift more cars. I switched the balance and now did more car trading than ceramic tiling.

A friend of mine had worked in his dad's restaurant and bar for years and he was now the manager of a nightclub in the town centre. Inevitably we became part of the furniture with regular partying.

My more relaxed lifestyle became a blessing and was making life wonderful. I also had plenty of time to visit my parents and always tried to be there whenever they needed anything. After about eighteen months of freedom I was finally getting readjusted and getting my mind back into a normal state. The wonderful present was erasing any pain and disturbance from the past. Blue skies and warm hearts heal all ills.

One thing that I could not yet do was stay indoors I always had to be out and about. It did not matter where I was going or what I was doing as long as I was in motion then I was happy, presumably it was an affect from the previous incarceration. One day I drove a friend down to Newcastle and decided to take the scenic route back up the A1. It was a beautiful sunny evening and I left the music off and the windows down and drove very slowly all of the way back up to Scotland taking in every part of the amazing scenery and wildlife. When I got to Edinburgh I put the windows back up then the music on and travelled along the M8 back to Glasgow.

Over the months I would drive all over Britain. My favourite trips were up into the Highlands of Scotland, no other country in the world has that combination of beauty mixed with atmosphere. You only have to slow down and you can sense the spirits of the ancient Highland people. I love driving up there and drinking in those energies.

Some nights I would drive past Loch Lomond and up to Lochgoilhead, I had tiled the bathrooms in some of the 'A' frame chalets up there in the late eighties and it still has a place in my heart even now. It is not a daytime spot for me it's at night when I like to visit. I park up, open my sunroof and just stare at the stars for hours. Light cancels out light so in the city very few stars are visible but only one hour north of Glasgow you can see the amazing blanket of millions of stars that appear to travel en masse across the sky in a wonderful sweep. It is a place where all of life's cares disappear for a while and you can travel anywhere in time or space if you have a good enough imagination and if you seek then you can also find answers and solutions within the silence and the majesty of the heavenly decorations.

One part of Scotland that I don't like is Glencoe, it has a bad air about it for me. Perhaps because I have Donald's and MacDonald's in my ancestry. Thankfully that is only a tiny spot in the vast garden that is there for all of us to enjoy. Scotland is a wonderful place.

Eventually I decided that a longer trip would be a good experience so I mapped a route for a nice long run. One of my friends has worked abroad during his entire career and at that time he was down in Albania. Again I don't want to reveal his identity either. All will become clear later on. Every time that I had gone abroad in the past was by air. Even half a day flying over to America was not much of a buzz so this time I would do a road trip and would get a picture and a sense of the energy over every inch of my travels. At that time it was dark grey winter and had been raining non-stop in Glasgow, I had certainly picked a good time to leave. I paid a visit to my nearest and dearest and told them that I was off on a solo run and would see them all in a few weeks.

I set off travelling light as always. Even driving on a motorway is a pleasure to me after so long sitting still. I reached the north of England and spent a few days with some friends then was off again and reached Dover at night. By the time I got over to Calais it was late night so I found a cheap hotel and went straight to bed.

In the morning I took a drive up to Dunkirk, it was strangely surprising to find a large town where I had always only pictured a beach covered in soldiers. After just a short visit I left and drove blindly and found a classic looking French district. I parked up and walked along the road to a small café. None of them could speak English and they made it clear that they were not happy with me for making no effort to speak French, how could I explain that I come from Glasgow where we don't speak very good English never mind another foreign language. I used sign language to order some food and drink and got there in the end.

Next I set off back down past Calais and past the edge of Paris, I had been warned to avoid the crazy Parisian streets. I was tempted to travel to the birthplace of the writer Henri Charriere in the Ardeche but I had a friend in Lyon and had already promised to stop in and visit him so I gave the Ardeche a miss. The atmosphere in Lyon was nothing like northern france, down here it had a bit of a mediterranean air with a lawless edge to it. There was a large amount of shadey characters and not the respectable type these were the real bandits and street rats who would open your neck for the price of a meal. The local police all had the look of a murderer about them which was very disconcerting. This was definitely not the place for me.

I only lasted one night at my friend's house and decided to set off again as soon as I woke up and that happened to be at 4 am. I had a shower then quietly went through and woke my friend taking care not to wake his wife and told him that I was leaving. "You are going so early, why?" He asked. "I'm working on my intuition for this whole trip so onwards it is." I answered. "Next time then my friend." He said. "Next time." I smiled and I was away.

I travelled across towards Italy and drove through the series of tunnels in the Alps. It was a wet grey morning in france and at one point the thick cloud had cleared and I could see large terraced houses perched on the mountain above the entrance to one tunnel, they stood there defiant as if they were part of the rock.

At last I reached a battered and unkempt tunnel that had dust and light rubble over the road and even had flickering lights. Italy. Very relaxed even here just a few feet over the border. It was a stark contrast to most of france which has a slightly authoritarian air. Sunlight reached in through the end of the last tunnel and I noticed that it was almost 8am, I emerged out and into bright sunshine which was made all the more amazing by the dark and wet france that I had just left. Now that the sun was on the way up it would no doubt be just as nice over on the French side, I had just been lucky enough to time it perfect and catch the transition.

I pulled in at the first service station and was happy to discover that it was very warm outside even at this early hour. The scenery here was barren so I bought something to drink then set off again until I found a small town. While the French had seemed a bit too serious and not very friendly, the Italians had a more relaxed attitude. They all had a co-conspirator look about them, not a sneaky one, more of a tough guy air. Even the women had a masculine energy about them. I sat drinking cold orange juice and observed. I was not looking to score with any birds I was only into a bit of RW style ornithology. There was a large amount of well turned out ladies yet while they would look great in a photo, that tough spirit which they had about them was not my taste and I wonder to this day what could have caused it. I love women more than anything in the world and here I could not see many who had the feminine qualities that attract me. Perhaps it was the close proximity to the border that left only those with the strongest characters and genetics?

Back in the car my cd player got stuck on a Pink Floyd album and it stayed that way for weeks into the future. Whenever I hear any of the tracks today I am instantly transported back to that journey. I travelled across the north. Northern Italy is a beautiful part of the world and even from the motorway I was surprised at the scenery and the calm atmosphere that blankets the entire country. There were also some nice houses dotted along the way with perfect scenery around them, an estate agents dream land, Mother Nature has already done the work.

In my younger years I was mad for designer clothes and I would never have been able to drive near Milan without at least a window shopping trip. A bit older and wiser I could now see all of that as foolishness. I still bought a few bits of good designer gear, mostly Armani purely because it looks good and is well made but I had become just as happy with cheap casual clobber and the labels made no difference. The journey up to Milan was out of the way so I gave it a miss.

In familiar regions I always drive with no more than a quarter tank of petrol to maximise miles per gallon (a lighter car goes further for your pound). On this journey I had no clue where the next station would be so I made a habit of filling up to the brim at every service station.

I was tempted to pull off at Verona to see some Juliets but I was tired from my 4 am rise and the almost constant travelling. My plan had been to drive across northern Italy then down the east coast to Bari in the far south and catch a ferry over to Greece and judging by the beautiful scenery up here it would have been great if I was not in need of sleep. I checked my atlas and noted a port at Venice, if it did not have a ferry going to Greece then it would surely have one going down to Bari so I headed straight for Venice.

My tiredness hampered me and I managed to take a wrong road into lost territory and had to pull in at a service station. No one could speak English so I had to get off the motorway and find a hotel. After some stress I found one and parked up. The woman at the desk was an absolute stunner, she had the classic Italian beauty but she also had that magical feminine spirit. She perked me right up. I asked her for directions from there to the road to Venice and she was very helpful and good natured. I then asked if I could pay to use a phone and she let me use one for free, every penny saved is good.

I called my friend in Albania and he again told me to drive down the coast for the scenery and experience but I explained that I was too tired had lost my motivation and just wanted to get to his house. He assured me that there was a ferry that went from Venice to what sounded like Izoobenitsa in Greece. This was good news and I told him that I would be there sooner than planned. I thanked the woman and left the hotel.

Driving fast I flew along towards Venice ignoring the scenery. I was struggling to stay awake and almost hit another car at a roundabout. Trying to stay awake read the map read the road signs and avoid the other cars was spoiling my fun. I had no wish to take a trip into Venice proper I just wanted to find the port and get into a cabin where I could sleep for a while.

I have almost died five times in my life and while that is a large amount for anyone it gets bizarre when you consider that every time has involved water and almost drowning.

None of it was to do with my swimming ability, my last dice with death came when I crashed my car off an icy country road in winter it careened across the edge of a field flew off an embankment and landed nose down in the waters of an icy burn. The car was stood on end and the freezing water started to pour in. Luckily I always wear a seatbelt and it was a four door so I climbed up onto the dashboard and out of the back door where I stood on the back end and jumped into darkness and landed on the bank. That was the fifth terrible experience around water so it was probably wise for me to avoid a city of water such as Venice.

At the port I went to the booking office and was delighted to find that there was a ferry that went to Igoumenitsa in Greece it departed in a few hours and there was a space so I paid up phoned my friend with my destination time put the paper sign in my windscreen, joined the queue and went for a nap. The guy behind me battered his car horn repeatedly as if his life depended on it, that woke me up and I found that I was holding back the queue. Why he couldn't have just tapped on my window I don't know. He was still giving me the bad eyes when we parked in a lower deck of the ferry. A porter carried my bag to the cabin and I was not sure of the trend so I gave him ten euros. He took it casually so I must have been correct.

I went straight to bed and later on was vaguely aware of a rumble from the massive engines. Next stop Greece. I slept soundly and in the morning walked about the ferry. It was big and was covered in poor looking people sleeping on the open deck and on landings. Presumably someone was doing a cheap rate deal with no cabin. The diesel smoke from the engines had a strong smell and whenever one of the people who slept on the deck came near you could smell that smoke mixed in with their sweat. I could not tell what country they came from, they were all able bodied and working age so I guess that they were poorly paid people coming to or from work.

Later on that day I went for a meal, there was a fast food style feeding area in the middle of the ship and a good restaurant up at the front. I walked along there for some decent food. The people up at this end did not smell of diesel that's for sure, most of them looked well off and in particular there was a young German couple both very tall and good looking well dressed and with an air of proper wealth about them. It was interesting to observe this crowd in contrast to the workers at the back.

The waiter was a Greek and when I ordered Scottish Salmon he laughed, "But you are from Scotland yes?" He said. "Yes I am."

"You come all of the way here and you want to eat a fish from Scotland!" He laughed again. "And I'm a Pisces, a bit fishy eh." I said. "What?" He asked confused. "The Salmon is the best choice here." I smiled. "But you must try something else." He said in a friendly way. "I'll try some greek coffee later on."

The fish was nice and when I came back from the restaurant the sun was shining so I spent most of the day sitting outside on a bench soaking up the rays. It was late evening when I disembarked at the greek port of Igoumenitsa. I phoned my friend and told him that I had made a mistake, the ferry was travelling on to another port so I had been given the wrong arrival time and was now here early. I asked for directions to Albania but he told me that it was too hard to follow and said that he would still come down to meet me. Like a fool I forgot to ask how long he would be and it was eight long hours before he appeared.

We drove off through the roads of northern Greece. The scenery was dull and I was numb from the wait yet I did like the atmosphere. By the time we reached his place it was daylight again. He had a nice house with good views in a reasonably clean district. I slept for a couple of hours before he took me out for a tour. The country was in a mess and had serious problems. Many of the people were painfully poor, malnourished and were dressed badly. My friend would not have gone anywhere near this region if there was not a wage to be had. He has always had itchy feet and goes out of his way to find jobs in faraway countries. The sunshine was good and I relaxed.

He lived comfortably enough and was on top of his game. Most of his spare time was spent over the border in Greece where many people speak english and the country is far more civilised than it's neighbour. I borrowed my friend's car and cruised about his part of Albania. Even here I could not sit still and had to be on the move. He had a two door convertible and I had some fun catching the sun while I chased the best performance out of the engine on the dusty roads.

His job kept him up to his neck all week so it was the weekend before he took me over to Greece. We travelled over the border and far down to a good spot where we parked up at a bar and I did some observing. I found that the Greeks shared some similarities with the Italians, the men were friendlier though and not as menacing and the women like their Italian cousins were more masculine than our Scots birds yet the Greeks had a feminine grace not unlike that of big cats of the jungle. They moved with a flowing style and that was nice to survey. I enjoyed the atmosphere of these learned people with their warrior history. The visits were too short and I vowed to come back for a long holiday rather than just a trip. I had been to Corfu for a couple of weeks in the past but it was a party where we bounced from bars to bed the whole time so I never got a feel for the energy. A full tour of Greece was definitely on the cards in the future.

For now I decided that I had come far enough east. I stayed for some weeks keeping my friend company and meeting his girlfriend, a workmate from the Ukraine. She was beautiful intelligent and interesting, he was certainly doing well. Eventually I felt that it was time to return to my homeland.

When I was planning the journey home I suddenly had the urge to carry on with the adventure and drive all of the way down to Australia. I looked at the atlas and found that some countries on the way were no good so it would be more sea than road. It could be done and experiencing the far east then Australia would be an amazing trip. In the end I ignored my instincts put the visit off for a future date and decided to come home to Scotland.

I told my friend that it was time for me to go, I noticed that my presence had given him itchy feet again and he promised to come back to Scotland for a visit. "Until next time." I said. "Next time tiler, soon I hope." He answered. My trip was over and I started my journey home.

7 Tarawoo

I snuggled into the warm embrace of the friendly atmosphere in Glasgow and my energy levels leapt up and remained high. It was great to see the Scottish swagger again where both males and females stroll confidently along. We Scots have an open friendly air, happy to help anyone yet equally we have a wild spirit and are just as happy to fight anyone if provoked and our women are definitely sexier than most others. I absolutely love them.

It was wonderful to see my nearest and dearest again with visits and even chance meetings. The weather had improved so Glasgow was looking good. There is nothing like a trip away to make you fall in love with your homeland again.

Back at work I persuaded my partners to start doing interest free credit deals on our cars. Most of our customers struggled to put a grand together but they could all afford to pay £50 per week for twenty weeks or so. It was the right move and the cars started shifting really well. As long as we sold enough cars then we could not lose, we would always be floating from the payments.

A friend offered me a partnership to work with him refurbishing flats but it would be full time so I had to give the idea some thought first. Within one week I received two more offers to work on other legitimate projects and I considered it all.

I had now fully adjusted to the real world, the painful memories were all buried deep and I was doing well spiritually and mentally. The future was also looking bright financially. Every minute out in the world is an amazing experience for me. I was still travelling everywhere unable to sit still and it was all good and enjoyable. I had wonderful people about me and that is the best cure for anything.

On the 3rd of May 2002 I had a big kitchen floor to finish tiling and also had to meet my friend who was laying a wooden floor as a free favour for me. I was parked in University avenue just off Byres road in the west end of Glasgow. My car was parked facing the kerb, it was a beautiful morning with a nice breeze and some sunshine.

I sat in my car and started the engine when suddenly another car skidded to a halt behind mine blocking me in. I knew straight away that this was grief but I could never have imagined just how much. I jumped out and four men shot out of the other car. They all had a shifty look about them so I knew that this was not to be a fight, they were clearly plain clothed police. "What do you want?" I called to them as they all rushed towards me.

"We will tell you in a minute! Keep your hands at your sides! Turn round! Give us your hands behind!" They snatched at my arms and rattled handcuffs onto my wrists. I was scared and tried to get my brain working, what can this be? I don't want to go back to jail, I've still got seventeen months left on that old parole licence is that what they are after to screw me on that? I've been free for two years and have kept my nose clean what are they up to?

"What do you want?" I asked again despondent now but not anywhere near ready for their reply. "William gage we are detaining you on suspicion of the MURDER of justin macalroy... my legs went weak and their evil words faded away into a deep sound tunnel.

Why were these bastards pulling me for a murder? They frog marched me over to their car and shoved me in the back. It made no sense and I realised that it was all a ploy. They would scare me with the murder nonsense in order to get me to admit to leaving the country a couple of times and trading used cars and all while I was out on parole licence and had not informed my parole officer.

The prospect of being locked up again in another hellhole jail for the last seventeen months of my parole time was terrifying and I had to get my mindset out of the wonderful world of freedom and love and go straight back into the justice system world of evil and hate and treachery and danger. I once again faced a battle for survival against the forces of darkness. Even being in a car close to such wicked souls was extremely uncomfortable and brought sick into my throat. Evil comes off CID police like steam from a kettle and if like me you are sensitive and perceptive to people's energies then it is disgusting to experience.

These coppers told me that they were from the south side of Glasgow and asked me to give them directions to the nearest police station which was Partick. Like a clown I actually gave them the directions. Looking back on it they must have known already and were playing some sort of psychological game on me. I was so numb with shock that I couldn't see through the agonising waves of stress that were swamping my senses.

They got me to partick police station and pushed me into a side room where they strip-searched me. They put me in a cell for a couple of minutes then two new CID came to collect me. I was taken to an interview room and immediately I could tell by their manner and facial expressions that they were actually going to have a dash at me for a crime that I had not committed. And it was a murder.

Normally I would remain silent but I was so shocked and stressed and terrified that I answered some questions. I was naturally very evasive when it came to revealing too many details about my used car trading because I had to protect other innocent people from these devils.

I admitted that in the past few months we had sold more than a dozen cars. They specifically asked me if I had sold a white car and I refused to say. When they asked me for the names and addresses of my trade partners and my nearest and dearest I absolutely refused and told them that I was being evasive because I had been unlucky enough to learn the nature of police already so I had every reason therefore not to trust them and did not want maniac police terrorising my people. I told them that I did not mean a personal insult to them in particular I was just wary of all police in general. One of them protested and said that the two of them were straight. I replied that his colleague beside him right now could have been up to no good last night and would hardly tell anyone about it so even he could not trust his pal never mind me trust any of them. History has proven that most police are corrupt not just a minority of them. I later learned that sure enough at that precise moment they were crashing through doors and terrifying my loved ones who have never been involved in any crime in their life.

I have no idea why these two were asking me these questions when they clearly already had the information. All of the questions were about me and my friends and family not about a murder and that was a sign that I was to be fitted into the crime rather than the other way about. After two hours one of them said, "Lets have a comfort break." They had just snatched me off the street for a crime that I did not commit then subjected me to two solid hours of psychological torture questioning. What kind of person could then use the term 'comfort break'?

They took me back to the cell and I paced up and down like a caged Tiger, four steps one way then spin and four steps back continually. This was a nightmare and was made worse because I had personally seen many innocent people in every jail that I had been in. Most of the injustice cases were for murder, a crime which puts the police under the most pressure to get results by any means.

The police and the crown prosecutors are not a machine they do make mistakes and what is most terrifying is that they very often do it on purpose just to clean up their crime statistics. And whether it has been done on purpose or not they always do everything to hide the truth and keep the victims locked up for as long as possible. It is all about keeping the public blind to the malevolence and evil that is the heart and culture in our police stations and courts.

After just a few minutes they took me back to the interview room where they battered into me again with non-stop questions which all appeared innocuous but I could see clearly that they were intended to gather information that could be used against me maliciously. Not evidence of any crime just information that would allow a sneaky prosecutor to pretend to be an authority on my life to know everything about me and so appear to be speaking with learned knowledge when he accused me of the crime of murder.

I continued to answer some questions and remained adamant and would not reveal any specific details to them because they could not be trusted. I repeatedly told them that I was innocent, I had never murdered anyone and so my personal details would not help them to catch a killer that I did not even know.

They again asked about a white car and if I had bought or sold one in my capacity as a used car trader. Again I refused to say. Why help two rats who were looking very much like they were determined to set me up by any means? This time they pulled out a set of clothes, all splash-proof gear very similar to the stuff that we wear when we are jet washing the cars at my friend's yard however this stuff that the police had was much thinner and was partly melted in places yet perfectly clean and untouched elsewhere as if someone had been at them with a lighter. In particular the gloves were ski type and while the nylon was partly melted on the outside at one or two places, the exposed lining inside was completely untouched and still bright white. A naked flame would have melted the inside or at least made it brown or black. Only a flame carefully held away at a distance would cause such minimal damage because the melted parts were on both sides! Had someone been dickying them up with a lighter?

They asked me if I had ever worn those clothes and I answered honestly and said no. The questioning went on for another two hours until they smashed my heart with this, "The reason that we've been asking you about that white car is because one was abandoned on the night five minutes after the murder and those clothes that we showed you were found inside. We also found firearm discharge residue and your DNA on the clothes."

"What! How can it be? I've never worn those clothes. How can my DNA be on them?" I exploded with fright. "You tell us." They said and right then behind their smug smiles I could see that they were happy to abuse their power over life and death.

DNA is the holy grail of modern day fit ups. You could do a poll of any amount of people, tell them that you are a prosecutor and they have to be the juror, tell them that the defendants DNA has been found and ask them if they can give you a quick answer whether he is likely to be guilty. Most will say that he is likely to be guilty and that will be without considering the ease with which DNA can be planted. That automatic response is thanks to years of media brainwashing with undiluted propaganda about billion to one DNA and trustworthy police.

To see the full power of media mind warping you only have to look at America. In the run up to the illegal Iraq war the American media swamped the people with so much misinformation that to this day 87% of Americans believe that Saddam Hussein was behind the twin towers attack on 9/11. Visit alexjones.com for more info.

In that police station I knew that I was in serious trouble. Since the coppers had gone as far as making a false claim about my DNA being on a set of clothes that I had not worn then who knows what else they had done against me. Even my most terror stricken thoughts at that point could not grasp the enormity of the catalogue of blatantly criminal actions that would later come to light.

Crucially they had been questioning me for a total of four hours now and not once had they accused me of being the killer and not once had they asked me any normal questions, they were all clearly intended to gather information that could be twisted. Next they asked me if I knew how the victim had been killed and when I said 'no' they said, 'we can tell you that he was shot dead'. Why would they need or want to tell me that if I was meant to be the killer? Strange people. They charged me with the murder of Justin Macalroy. I am innocent and I reasoned that despite the false claim of my DNA and despite whatever else they had been up to I would prove my innocence and get back home to the free world where I belong.

Up until this point I had been terrified and confused and was trying to analyse every word, every facial expression, every inch of those clothes and every bit of energy in the air. Now that they had charged me I could see that they could not care less about innocence. They were determined to convict me for a murder that was committed by someone else. They were walking me back to the cell when my fear was replaced by anger. I was raging mad at their audacity and the injustice and I had the urge to smash the pair of them. I tensed up as we walked along and turned to the nearest one, "You fucking bastards!" I growled. He looked incredulous, "What?" He asked innocently. "Your setting me up for a murder." My teeth were gritted now and I eyed his jawbone, it was ripe for a crack. "We don't do that sort of thing anymore, that all happened in the seventies when everyone was mad." He said with apparent sincerity. He was either a complete moron or an extremely good liar. I realised that these two could well be innocent, their boss could have convinced them that I was guilty. I decided that these bams were only minions and I would be wasting my time. When I was back in the cell pacing I thought it over deeply and decided that however justified it may be, violence was not the way to win this fight for my life. I must try to win it using peaceful and legal means. I vowed to stay true to that idea no matter what came up during this case I would try not to lose my patience or threaten or harm anyone even when they were at it. I would try to use their crimes against them rather than make them the victims.

Every single minute of every day of the rest of the battle is an absolute horror. It exhausts me to even think about it and I don't want to go into details too deeply. I could fill five hundred pages with it however I don't want any of you to read it and even remotely feel the pain that I have suffered. It is too horrific to fully describe on these pages and is too ugly to put into your minds. Even a skeleton of the story will make your stomach churn. Therefore I will condense the following to protect you from too much poison.

I was removed from partick police station and taken all of the way over to Hamilton station where I was kept for four days over a bank holiday weekend. They had a police dog barking continually somewhere behind and below the level of my cell. Next I was remanded to the hellhole Barlinnie jail. I had last been in there six years ago and there was now a large number of social workers, their presence prevented the screws from battering and torturing the prisoners as much as they used to. There remained a distinct air of menace about most of the screws and a well practised technique of psychological torture with flashes of occasional violence so the oppression was almost as bad and the environment was just as destructive and counter to any rehabilitation ideas or practices. The brutal jail regime was still designed and determined to make the prisoners worse thus guaranteeing money for the true crooks well into the future.

Family contact is well known to be an essential and major factor in keeping prisoners sane and positive enough to ever even contemplate going straight yet the screws in Barlinnie and Glenochil treat the innocent visitors like wild animals. They subject them to hours of unnecessary waiting and to open hostility, psychological pressure and very limited physical contact with partitions between the visit seats, all intended to destroy family units and all done under the guise of the so called war on drugs. Anyone who has been in any jail in Scotland will tell you that the screws and governors have licensed informers who they supply with heroin to flood the jails. There is never a dry up of drugs in jail because the SPS absolutely guarantee the supply. There have even been leaks where grasses have claimed that the old governor of Barlinnie would work with the drug squad who would clear all routes to ensure that the gear never ran out. That may be true. Yet they use the drug problem as an excuse to terrorise innocent members of the public who's loved ones happen to have fallen foul of the law. It is a disgusting state of affairs. Don't just take my word for it, ask people who have been there.

Do the maths. At that time there were over one thousand prisoners in Barlinnie and more than nine hundred were heroin addicts who were using it to escape the torture and all were steaming drunk every week and many were off their nut every single day. There were less than fifty jail dealers and they did not walk in carrying kilos of gear (neither do visitors) so the supply comes from somewhere else. Where else? You are left with only the governors and screws. What do the SPS do to people who deal drugs in jail? Do they target and isolate them? Yes they do but if they are grasses (and 99 out of 100 are) then the SPS ignore the dealing and actually give their pals extra privileges. You work it out.

I had a visit from my solicitor Bob Kerr, he told me that the murder victim Justin Macalroy had been involved with politicians. A police officer claimed that Justin Macalroy's dad Tommy Macalroy had contacted his friend the MP Frank Roy and offered him money to pressure the police to arrest anyone in order to get his sons body back and laid to rest. It had been two months since Justin Macalroy was murdered and the police could not or would not find the killer so it seems that Tommy Macalroy used his pull with the politicians to get someone arrested and stitched up in order to stop the police from keeping the body at the morgue for years while they were unable to make a move on the actual killer. I cannot state that as fact of course until we get evidence it is hearsay. It did explain a lot of things.

The MP Frank Roy shared an office in Wishaw with the (then) First Minister of Scotland Jack McConnell. Months later the Sunday Times revealed that Tommy Macalroy and Justin Macalroy were suspected heroin barons and had been under surveillance by the SDEA for the past four years. They had been followed to Estonia where they met some of their pals who were later arrested while trying to smuggle millions of pounds worth of heroin back to Scotland. The Macalroy's were never arrested yet their associates all spent the next half decade in jails in Scotland and Estonia. While in jail one of those pals admitted (or claimed) that the Macalroy crew were all MI5 sanctioned workers and all had a heroin trading licence. Their crew had only been caught because their Russian mafia partners had been under surveillance, and it was not the SDEA protect your dealers style, this was the real thing and when the time came the foreign police made a move and arrested the players. The Scottish authorities including the SDEA had apparently refused to give any evidence or details about the Macalroy's to the Estonians. Tens of millions of pounds in taxpayers money wasted by the establishment following the Macalroys for four years just to pretend to be fighting a war on drugs because when they had the chance to actually jail them the decision was made to Protect them by withholding evidence! Is that accurate? Perhaps Justin Macalroy was innocent, he had no job yet he did have a large detached house in the south of Glasgow and he also had a Porsche Carrera, a Mercedes ML Jeep, and an Audi TT. Perhaps his dad Tommy Macalroy is not a licensed informer. He is said to have had ten million in money and assets seized after the murder and the police one day decided to give it all back. No proceeds of crime cases against the chosen few of the round table. I have been told by a number of people that Tommy Macalroy is indeed a licensed informer and one guy in particular told me that Tommy Macalroy has been stitching people up and getting them jailed since 1978. That all seems to be true and it would explain a lot of things. While all of it is hearsay and gossip I have yet to hear or see anything contrary to it so I am left with little choice but to believe it.

The Sunday Times went on to say that the (then) First Minister of Scotland Jack McConnell, the (then) Home Secretary of the UK John Reid, the Wishaw MP frank Roy, numerous other Labour party big wigs and a number of senior spies and police all attended a dinner inside Tommy Macalroy's country club on the 3rd of March 2002.

Jack McConnell and Frank Roy apparently shared a table with the Macalroy's while the SDEA sneaked about still keeping the Macalroy's under surveillance. When the media got wind of the fact that the Macalroy's had slipped ten thousand pounds in cash to Jack McConnell he had his secretary jailed for handling that money! What the public servants were all doing socialising with suspected heroin barons has never been established. The Macalroys were believed to be so high up the heroin baron chain that they were kept under full SDEA surveillance for four years. The (then) First Minister of Scotland jack McConnell was asked what they were all up to at that dinner and he claimed that the surveillance operation on the Macalroys was so important that it could not possibly be jeopardised by refusing to go to the Macalroy's dinner. It was so important that the entire top ranks of Scottish Labour, our spies and police were all allegedly willing to risk a massive media exposure and backlash and the embarrassment rather than put that surveillance job at risk. The gunman struck just four days after that dinner. When we asked for the SDEA film footage which would show the actual killer with Justin Macalroy and would prove my innocence they said that the surveillance had been removed 48 hours before the murder! So either the SDEA were there and do have film footage which would clear me or the surveillance had actually been removed just two days before Macalroy was shot. If it is the latter then Jack McConnell's excuse as to why he and so many other establishment figures were socialising with suspected MI5 licensed heroin barons is a lie. Whatever the truth is, the public deserve to know. We all deserve to see a full public inquiry with a judge forcing Jack McConnell and every other witness to give evidence under oath. The people deserve to see the truth.

Bob Kerr later came to me and said that Tommy Macalroy had contacted the prosecutor in my case and 'asked' him to ask Bob Kerr and me to sign a form that would release the Mercedes Jeep and the Audi TT from the police garage. One had a bullet hole and they were both at the scene of the crime therefore could potentially have forensic evidence which the defence could use. I asked Bob Kerr how a suspected heroin baron could have the audacity to ask a prosecutor in a murder case to release cars that could hold forensic evidence and what had possessed the prosecutor to go ahead and help him?

Also you could be held on remand for a maximum 110 days

in Scotland before trial so the cars would be released in three months and would not have lost much value by then. I look back now and wonder whether Tommy Macalroy knew more about my future than I did because the 110 days was soon gone and those cars were released without my permission. How can a suspected heroin baron tell a prosecutor what to do and actually persuade that prosecutor to break the law and throw away potential evidence in a murder case? What is Tommy Macalroy? How can he have such power and influence over public servants?

The police released my age to the media and it was printed, I was 31 at the time. Next they took me to an id parade. They told me that everyone would be wearing racing driver style masks that covered the hair and neck but not the face. There were 10 witnesses, 8 wanted to see the faces half covered by the mask and 2 wanted to see the full face. It was a bizarre request and Bob Kerr told me that it was iffy but that we should go through and see what happens. I agreed however I insisted that Bob Kerr be allowed to take the mask away with him, I did not want the police to use it in another set up once I had worn it. With no public about and no one to pretend to they laughed and agreed. It is amusing for them when they privately admit to being corrupt. When we walked through for the parade we were both amazed at the spectacle. There were six wee boys in the line up and one of them was even a dark skinned Asian and another had a bum fluff beard. They all then pulled the masks up to cover half of their faces but you could see the clear eyes and unblemished skin, it was obvious that they were all little teenagers. Bob Kerr and the police walked through a doorway and I stood staring at the line of boys. To put me there was like placing a big Alsatian dog beside six cats then asking the postman to pick out the dog that bit him. It was an outrageous and blatant attempt to manufacture false identification evidence and what was really shocking was that they were doing it brazenly in front of my solicitor and me, that got me very worried about what the hell they had been up to when we were not there. I was terrified and raging mad all at once and I stormed through the unlocked door to the witness end where Bob Kerr and the police were standing. I never gave them the chance to protest, I looked at the CID officer who appeared to be running the parade, "You cant be serious about this id parade." I growled angry about their audacity.

Bob Kerr joined in and turned to them, "He does have a point, how old are these boys?" He asked.

The CID officer asked the boys to call out their age. Five were only 17 and one was 18. "The oldest one is 13 years younger than me and my age has already been printed in the papers." I said angrily.

The smarmy rat smirked and said, "Well I think it's a fair line up, one of them is almost as tall as you."

I could not take it, this copper was openly setting me up right in front of my face. I lunged forward intending to crack his jaw. Bob Kerr was closer to him than me and he jumped in my way and grabbed my arms. "Leave it." He said quietly. I did not struggle, he is a decent guy and I did not want to fall out with him. "This parade is a farce I cannot allow my client to take part in it." He said forcefully then shoved me back through the doorway. I took off the mask and gave it to Bob Kerr saying, "Here's a souvenir to remind you of the corruption of Strathclyde police." He took it and nodded. The line of boys stared at us silently, no doubt they had been equally surprised to be put in a line up that defied all sanity.

The police were not for giving up, they rushed out and got a mannequin then dressed it up in the half melted clothes that they had shown me and had claimed to have found my DNA and gunpowder residue on. Those clothes had never been kept in evidence bags and people had actually seen the jacket on the floor in a police station.

Tracy Macalroy the widow of the deceased Justin Macalroy was six months pregnant at that time and was understandably in a terrible state. They had spent many days with her and had managed to convince her that I was the guilty man and that she would be put in front of me at an id parade. They made her wait for hours and when she showed clear signs of exhaustion they told her that it was time to be brought face to face with the murderer who had shot her husband but not to worry because they would protect her from the dangerous animal. All of that when Bob Kerr, the wee boys and I were all long gone hours ago. They walked her along an unlit corridor and let the fear and tension build right up then suddenly flung open a door and shoved her in front of them into a brightly lit room. Just two steps inside she was immediately confronted by the mannequin which was facing her and was dressed up and masked up with only its bright blue eyes showing and it even had a black bag crushed in its hand to represent a gun. She was understandably terrified and jumped back. They then told her that the clothes on the mannequin were the gunman's clothes and asked her to sign the police labels.   Five other witnesses were later shown those clothes and all said that they were nothing like the gunman's clothes. The false identification of those clothes and the circumstances surrounding the mannequin are typical of corrupt police tactics. There were not six mannequins with six sets of similar clothes and they did not use the id parade room with the glass partition. Also Tracy Macalroy had already made two statements saying that she had not seen the gunman clearly enough to identify him or his clothes. Stitched up to the max. Scottish justice.

Next they produced a photo of a line of big white cars and it looked on the face of it a bit too fair. They then claimed that one witness had picked out the white car that had been abandoned and said that it was 'similar' to the gunman's car. Later we learned that the line up of white cars was only for the photograph, the false witness in question CB had previously said that he did not see anything and after police pressure he said that he saw a red car and eventually they showed him one white car on it's own and told him to sign a statement saying that it looked like the gunman's car (that he had not seen!). Next they got his dad IB to say that he had also seen a similar white car near his house in Cambuslang early on in the afternoon on the day of the murder.

Next in a bizarre episode two Special Branch officers from Belfast terrorised an old friend of mine and tried to quiz him but he had no information for them. What were they doing involved in a Glasgow murder case? Again we desperately need a public inquiry into every aspect of this outrage.

The police had terrorised most of my family and friends and on two separate occasions they told different people that they knew for certain that Mr N (my friend who had robbed the jewellers with me some years ago) was the killer and that I was driving the car. Every witness at the scene had described the gunman as being 5' 10' tall and athletic. Mr N fits that description exactly whereas I don't because I am over 6' tall. Also Mr N is a driver not me.

Weeks later in Barlinnie I was looking out of my cell window and there was Mr N he was in the hall opposite mine and was out walking in the exercise yard. I called out of my cell window to him and he smiled up when he recognised my voice. I knew that gangland murder was not his game either so I openly asked out loud, "Where were you on the 7th March at 10pm." He thought about it then called back, "I was in jail for fighting with a couple of coppers." I was happy to hear that his alibi was solid. "You are lucky mate they wanted to stitch you up with me! They claimed to be certain that you were the gunman. They must have eventually found out that you were in jail that night and with such an unshakable alibi they reluctantly took your name off the case." He was chalk white by now. Like everyone else in the system he knew how easy it is for the crown to take your life regardless of innocence. I was eventually moved over to that hall and he helped me to stay sane despite the pressure. I also made a new friend big T2000.

As already stated at that time in Scotland you would be held on remand before trial for 110 days and the law states that you must have equality of arms and be given access to all evidence before trial. My persecutors tortured the life out of me for Twenty-Two months on remand for a capital crime. They abused legal procedures to enable them to keep me locked up for that length of time and they blatantly broke the law throughout that period by withholding crucial evidence. In particular they refused to hand over copies of the footage from the 43 police CCTV cameras which proved that I was not at the scene of the crime, the white car was not there and amazingly two of the prosecution witnesses Steven Madden and his friend were not even there!

During almost two years on remand and faced with this disgusting catalogue of blatant corruption I wrote literally hundreds of protest letters begging for help and demanding fairness and justice. Altogether I wrote six (recorded delivery) letters to the (then) Lord Advocate of Scotland Colin Boyd. I told him that I was being set up and that he was using false witnesses and planted evidence against me and also crucial evidence was being illegally withheld from me by the Crown,

I begged him to investigate.

Colin Boyd completely ignored me and the crimes that had been and were being committed against me. Ultimately he perverted the course of justice by denying me access to the evidence that proved my innocence and by using false witnesses and planted evidence against me. His procurator fiscal was in possession of the CCTV footage which proved that at least two prosecution witnesses were not even at the scene yet Colin Boyd the Lord Advocate of Scotland still used them and kept the truth hidden from the jury. What chance has anyone got in Scotland if the top prosecutor himself is blatantly corrupt? How many innocent people did that man stitch up and lock up for life during his many years in the top job? How much agony has Colin Boyd created in the world?

I had parted company from the solicitor Bob Kerr and in a disastrous move I now had the solicitor advocate Jim Keegan of Keegan Smith solicitors in Livingston. Before the trial Jim Keegan told me that the Macalroy's solicitor Joe Shields had told him that the police had managed to convince the widow Tracy Macalroy that I was the one who had killed her husband and they had thus persuaded her to help them to convict the bogus guilty man by telling lies for them. She was now prepared to pick me out in court as the killer no matter what I looked like even though she had never seen me in her life and by her own account had not seen the gunman either just a dark figure.

I was now faced with planted DNA, a widow who was willing to commit perjury and identify me as the killer and three further witnesses who had been persuaded by the police to say that they were at the scene and witnessed the killer getting into a white car. I had no possible way to prove that the DNA was planted. I hoped that a reasonable jury would look at the conflicting statements of the witnesses and see that they get more ridiculous and more damning as they go along thanks to repeated visits by the police and so are clearly not safe. And I hoped that we would at last get our legal right to access to the CCTV footage which proved that at least two of the three false witnesses (who had been persuaded to say that they had seen a white car) were not even at the scene themselves.

I wrote protest letters detailing the stitch up case to the

Queen, the (then) Prime Minister Tony Blair, the (then) Home Secretary John Reid, the (then) First Minister of Scotland Jack McConnell, to all 134 MSP's in the Scottish parliament, the (then) Chief Constable of Strathclyde police William Rae, to every police Chief Superintendent and every police Superintendent in Scotland and I was completely ignored by all. I then wrote a desperate letter to the miscarriages of justice organisation and they did answer. While they could not help me due to the fact that I had not yet been tried, they did promise to keep an eye on my case.

After almost two years of absolute hell and torture where no one in the establishment would obey the law or act in any way sane, I was in a terrible state. On top of all of it was the hellish regime in Barlinnie jail where I was being kept locked up for 23 hours per day then on the brief minutes outside the cell was subjected to terror tactics with extreme contempt and often aggression from the screws who brutalise all remand prisoners to get them buttered up for the kangaroo courts. When my trial eventually was about to start we still did not have any access to the evidence that proved my innocence and my brain was now like porridge. I was in a real mess physically and psychologically and was finding it difficult to function. Even tying my shoelaces was hard to perform in my shattered mind, I was exhausted after so much torture. In other words I was exactly where they wanted me to be.

The trial started and the first false witness was Tracy Macalroy. She was clearly terrified about her task to tell lies and she cried whenever a question required a false answer. The prosecutor Alan McKay was happily perverting the course of justice by using planted evidence and false witnesses against me. He asked Tracy Macalroy what the gunman had been wearing. In her first two statements made before the police 'activities' she had not seen the gunman only a dark shadow from a distance and she could not id him or his clothes so Alan McKay had no right to ask her what the gunman's clothes were like however he is completely corrupt and knew that she had been persuaded to commit perjury for the crown so he was determined to bring out the false evidence in order to hoodwink the jury. Going against the interests of justice and the public he asked her about the gunman's clothes. She answered, "A big padded hood zip thing." It was clear that she was not very bright. I mean no disrespect to her I'm just stating the facts. Alan McKay could also see it so rather than ask her to describe the clothes in any further detail he got someone to hold up the partly melted cagoule from the mannequin. "Can you look at that jacket for me please". He asked.

Tracy Macalroy stared at it blankly. Alan McKay caught this and in a very sneaky move he did not ask if that was the gunman's jacket. First he said, "Can you look at the label on that jacket for me please." She looked at the manufacturers label and Alan McKay briefly let his eyes rush up to the ceiling in exasperation, "No, no the police label, look at that for me please." He asked and she did.

"Does that label have your signature on it?" He asked. "Yes." She answered. "Did you sign that label when you were inside Aitkenhead road police office?" She had only been there once and that was for the aborted id parade where she was ultimately confronted by the mannequin. Her eyes suddenly brightened as she realised at last that this was the jacket from the mannequin that they had told her was the gunman's jacket and that she had agreed to identify as such. Alan McKay caught her recognition and only now asked, "Is that the jacket that was worn by the man who shot your husband?"

"Yes." She lied and went into floods of tears. On that jacket they had planted my DNA and gunpowder residue. Next Alan McKay said "Have you ever seen the gunman or anyone resembling him since that night?" She went into floods of tears again and to the jury it seemed as though she was crying over her poor husband however it was fear at her job to lie. "Yes." She answered. "Where?" He asked. "Here." She said. "Here in this court!" Alan McKay said in a loud theatrically surprised tone. "Yes." She whispered through the tears. "Can you point him out to me please." He asked. She pointed over to me in the dock. "And what can you tell me do you recognise about him?" He asked. The mannequin had been almost completely covered with a hood and a scarf on its face. A genuine witness at the scene JW had described a completely different set of clothes to those on the mannequin and had noted a mask over his face, his eyes were shaded by the mask and the dark night. In contrast the mannequin that Tracy Macalroy had been confronted with had piercing blue eyes openly on display and I do have noticeable blue eyes however even if the gunman had blue eyes she would never have been able to see them under the mask at 10pm in the dark as he sprinted away from her house a full driveway length away from where she claimed to be and where another genuine witness said that she never was!

Despite the impossibility she said, "His eyes I remember starey eyes." The prosecutor asked her the height of the gunman. In later statements when she had claimed to have seen the gunman she agreed with every other witness that he was 5' 10'. In court she looked over at me and I slouch when I sit so it is impossible to guess my height when you have never seen me standing (as she never has) and she answered 'medium to tall' and the prosecutor smiled and carried on with the farce. I was sickened completely now, the monsters had taken a pregnant traumatised widow and somehow brainwashed her that they had the guilty man but that she would have to help them by telling some lies in order to get a conviction. Some of my people have since told me that they hate her for telling such lies however I make it clear to everyone that Tracy Macalroy is a victim not a perpetrator, she did commit perjury but it is the police who are guilty and in particular a Detective Sergeant John Ferguson, he should be in the dock not Tracy Macalroy. She did whisper at one point that she was not one hundred percent but that was skilfully ignored.

The next day I was declared guilty by the media. The rags ran stories with massive headlines EVIL EYES! THE KILLER HAD STAREY EYES! The stories made it sound as if Tracy Macalroy was a legitimate witness who had recognised me as having the same eyes as the killer. That was me now guilty in the minds of the public so anyone connected to the jurors could have influenced their deliberations from this skewed story. Later on in the trial one witness claimed to be the only person to see the gunman without his mask and this witness said that I was definitely not the guilty man, the media were silent about that! It should be illegal for the media to do such things because miscarriages of justice help to keep killers free.

My solicitor advocate Jim Keegan was completely useless. I

constantly tried to get him to do his job properly but I was in an exhausted psychological state and was not able to sack him and do the trial myself because I would not have been able to string one decent sentence together thanks to the almost two years of pre trial torture.

Two of the other false witnesses came in and refused to repeat the lies that they had apparently been forced by police to put in their statements. One of them said that the police had him under so much pressure that he signed anything just to get away from them. Alan McKay the prosecutor knew that these two witnesses were definitely false because he had access to CCTV footage which showed that they were not even at the scene. Yet he was happy to lie to the jury and use the false evidence. He did not let these two witnesses tell the truth, he shouted at them and gave each of them copies of their false statements and told them to get reading. He then read out loud their false statements to the jury. Every so often he would say, "Did you say that to the police?" And the witness could not say no because it is very dangerous to accuse police of being corrupt so they answer yes. Next he would say, "And is it the truth?" Again they had to say yes because otherwise they would be admitting to perjury. It was a complete farce and considering Alan McKay and his colleagues had actual irrefutable CCTV footage which proved that these statements were definitely not truthful this has to be one of the most serious crimes ever committed by a corrupt prosecutor in any court on the planet considering that it was all intended to take away the life of a man who was also not at the scene of the crime.

The prosecution then went on to spend two whole weeks talking crap and leading bogus witnesses. I have no idea why they did all of that, perhaps in an effort to exhaust the jury and make them believe that there was so much evidence to prove guilt that it took two weeks just to explain it. They led evidence about mobile phone calls in Easterhouse yet they had even dickied these up by removing calls out of the list in order to present a false picture about the user. Again Jim Keegan was useless.

The murder happened in Cambuslang in the South side of Glasgow not in Easterhouse in the East end. Almost every road in Easterhouse is covered by CCTV cameras so the crown illegally withheld the footage which proved that the white car which was found in Easterhouse was never anywhere near Cambuslang that night. They then based their entire case on the lie that the white car was used by the killer to travel from Cambuslang to Easterhouse. We have now learned that even the CCTV footage in Cambuslang shows that there was no white car at the scene and again the crown illegally kept that hidden from the defence and the jury.

We led defence evidence which proved that I was in the west end of Glasgow that night at 10pm. The corrupt prosecutor was determined to remove all truth from this kangaroo court and he did everything in his power and used every sneaky move in his fat book in an effort to bring doubt into the minds of the jury concerning my alibi evidence however we were telling the truth and the truth cannot be silenced. The jury perhaps were susceptible to the black magic of Alan McKay and his lies and sneaky techniques were powerful in the theatre of the courtroom.

Before the trial, throughout the remand period I had gone through thunderstorms of agony and uncertainty and was faced with an ever-changing prosecution case. At one point they claimed to have found a strand of my hair. I slipped a note to my solicitor and asked him to get the hair and check it because it would not have any gunpowder on it as I had not fired any guns. They came back and said, "Well it's not hair now, its DNA." They were changing the evidence as they went along in order to destroy any legitimate defence that I had so on a significant number of occasions I played them at their own game and gave many different tactics and explanations in the bugged lawyers rooms and over the bugged jail phones and in the bugged and filmed visit area. Ultimately though I did not lie to the police or the jury, I realised that the crown were the ones who were reliant on lies so as long as I stuck to the truth then I would eventually win one day. The truth is too powerful to be beaten therefore when they tell lies they are only temporarily putting off the inevitable. The truth will always come out in front, it is too bright and clean to be buried forever.

At the end of the trial the prosecutor echoed Tony Blair and said that the crown had put across a 'Powerful And Compelling Case' Blair had used those exact words when he was trying to persuade the people that his security services had given him a report that proved there were WMD's in Iraq. Jim Keegan was a nightmare, I should have shouted a passing jakey into the court and he would have done a better job of summing up despite not having seen the trial. The judge Lord Emslie summed up and he was fair and impartial, he told the jury to disregard Tracy Macalroy's evidence about the eyes because it would have been impossible for her to see the gunman's eyes under the big Eskimo hood which she had first described (during the initial stages of the police activities with her) and also the jacket from the mannequin was not identified by any witness including Tracy Macalroy in her first statements until she came to court and agreed with the prosecutor. Unfortunately her evidence about the eyes was powerful and even if the jury did not believe it they would have said to themselves that surely the widow of the deceased would not help the actual killer by telling lies to convict an innocent man therefore surely this man in the dock is the guilty one. That is why the police put so much effort into getting witnesses to lie especially if they are closely related to the victim, jurors are cynical and will convict on such 'hunches'.

Eleven months before the trial I had received a warning that a senior officer in Strathclyde police had boasted that police agents were going to be sneaked into my jury and their job would be to bully and confuse the genuine jurors in order to persuade and pressurise them to convict irregardless of the evidence heard at trial. I screamed about it in dozens of protest letters yet our corrupt legal system has such absolute power that they still seem to have went ahead with the plan because the jury came back with a shocking and disgusting guilty verdict which crushes my heart to this day.

They had found me not guilty of dumping the white car. They had clearly asserted that the so called DNA on the clothes could have been left there at any time by anyone. Also the car was 15 years old yet the crown were trying to pretend that there were no fingerprints or hairs or fibres or DNA anywhere on that car. They claimed that all they could find was my DNA on the clothes! Pure undiluted bullshit and the jury did acquit on that charge yet all that they were left with to tie me to the crime was the lies about the eyes from Tracy Macalroy and the trial judge himself had specifically told the jury to disregard that evidence. What brought them to convict me? There was no evidence left so they perhaps went on the hunch that the widow of the deceased would not condemn an innocent man. I had never seen or met Justin Macalroy or Tracy Macalroy in my life I had no motive whatsoever to meet him or speak to him or argue with him or kill him. His widow only tried to tell the lies because the corrupt police convinced her that I was somehow guilty, not because she knew anything that was not shown in court so the sickening reality is that I was convicted of a murder that I did not commit simply because a vulnerable widow had been convinced to tell lies by desperate corrupt police and she had in turn caused the jury to think outside the box and deny me the benefit of the doubt. Is that accurate?

If you were on that jury then please I beg you get in touch and let us know what the hell happened. Even if you only want to speak off the record, your verdict cost me my life and I think that I deserve to know. Please contact any of the following.

Aamer Anwar solicitors 63 Carlton Place Glasgow G5 9TW. Or call on
0141 429 7090. Ask for Mr. Anwar.

Paddy Hill M.O.J.O. Scotland 34 Albion St. Glasgow G1 1LH. Or call on 0141 552 7253. Ask for Paddy, John or Cathy.

Alex Neil MSP Scottish parliament Holyrood Edinburgh EH99 1SP. Or call on 0131 348 5703. Ask for Mr. Neil.

William Gage 2319 C3/15 H.M.P. Shotts Lanarkshire Scotland ML7 4LE. If you don't get an answer from me then please send your letter recorded delivery the SPS are notorious for keeping mail.

What would your verdict have been if the crown had not hidden the CCTV evidence from you? You would have seen that the white car was never in Cambuslang, it had never even left Easterhouse. And Steven Madden and his friend could not have seen a white car because the CCTV footage shows that they were not even there in that part of Cambuslang at that time. You can get life in jail for perjury in a murder trial so they did not tell those lies for fun. Steven Madden and his friend have mentioned in statements that they were pressured by police. It is clear to me that they were both forced to lie by the police.

Those same police claimed to have found my DNA and some gunpowder residue on the clothes from the white car. Yes they did get forensic scientists to talk about that evidence but lets face it any item could have been rubbed against the door handle of my house or car by the police before they gave them to the forensic people (that might explain the three unknown samples of DNA found on the clothes) equally the police corrupted everyone else so they could have just as easily got the forensic scientists to make false claims concerning DNA and gunpowder. Planting DNA and gunpowder is a million times easier and safer than corrupting people to act as false witnesses who were not even there and when CCTV footage exists that can expose the conspiracy. The police took extremely serious risks with those false witnesses, what would stop them from planting DNA and gunpowder?

What would your verdict have been if you had known the truth? I beg you please tell us. Even if you only want to communicate informally please tell us firstly what did happen and next what would have happened if you had known the truth. There is a corrupt law that prevents any juror from talking about what happened in the jury room. Firstly, you were lied to by the crown therefore my trial was not legitimate so that law cannot apply, and second I am more interested in what your verdict would have been if you had been given true facts. There is no law against such an answer, please help me.

After the devastating guilty verdict the prosecutor Alan McKay jumped up and told the judge that I had previous convictions of escalating violence and even firearms act offences. Thanks to the prosecutors and their exaggerated charges my two daft fights, the pepper spray and one robbery looked on paper like the crimes of a violent lunatic.

The judge sentenced me to Life imprisonment with a Minimum Twenty Years. I was completely destroyed by it all and was swamped with stress and agony and tunnel vision. I heard my amigo in the public gallery as he exhaled an agonised grunt when he heard the twenty year sentence, he knows that I am innocent and felt my pain. I stumbled down to the cells in a daze and was quickly taken back to Barlinnie. One of the prisoners who remained in the cells in court later told me that the police were all cheering and doing a dance after

I left and when two other police walked in and asked what they were celebrating they heard the answer that 'the gage just got twenty years' and these two started to laugh and cheer and join in the celebrations! What is wrong with these people? They seem to get an added thrill when they destroy the life of innocents.

'You have committed a couple of crimes in the past so we hate you and will delight if you suffer the ultimate injustice and lose your life.' Strathclyde's finest eh.

I was delivered into an empty filthy cell in Barlinnie and lay down like an old homeless dog, everything that is human had just been violently snatched out of me and I almost lost the will to live. I had just been sentenced to the rest of my life in prison for a crime that I did not commit and the very people who had done me knew that I was innocent all along and had illegally withheld the irrefutable CCTV evidence which proved my innocence. It has killed me all over again just trying to explain this outrageous case and the disgusting verdict. Absolute hell.

My nightmare and torture continues and it has been difficult to put this book together in between continued battles for my survival, no doubt the content has suffered to some degree as a result. Also this book will be sent straight to the printers without being edited. I need to keep the contents secret until the book is out and it is too late to stop me. I never underestimate the enemy. I have also had to write the bulk of this chapter very slowly one paragraph at a time and have missed out masses of further damning evidence which shows more of their blatant corruption. I had to do that in order to preserve my sanity, it is too horrific and far too painful to relive all over again as I attempt to write it here.

In Barlinnie I could not bring myself to phone all of my family and only managed to pluck up the courage to call my dad. He instinctively knew that I would not be able to handle their pain on top of mine at this early stage and he was thoughtful enough to stay calm and strong for me and that was a massive bonus. His unwavering strength reminded me of who and what I am and immediately my spirits began to lift. This was war and I had to stand up and fight for my life.

They had used their crooked legal system to take my life but I was determined to take it back so I started the process of fighting inside that system, I immediately launched an appeal. My loved ones were devastated after the trial of course and the appeal focused our energies yet it still took us a couple of months to get used to the shock and agony of this situation.

I was transferred to the maximum security Shotts prison in Lanarkshire. It was not a good feeling to be taken back in the gate that I had walked out of as a free man just four years ago. They put me in the NIC hall and my new cell looked straight over to my old cell in B hall, it was a painful view.

My torture of wrongful imprisonment had now gone on for two long years. Now that I had recovered a bit from the shock of the guilty verdict I thought over every part of the bogus trial and I believed that the solicitor advocate Jim Keegan had screwed me over and had helped the prosecution. Jim Keegan was busy promising my family and the guys at MOJO that he would absolutely get me out on appeal and they all believed him. When I voiced my concerns about him they all assumed that I was being a bit paranoid. Paranoia and cynicism are collective ailments among the incarcerated but the events and facts justified my fears and opinions. The truth is often too much for most people to face.

Only now that the trial was over did Jim Keegan let me see the witness statements that had been taken by the police. I could not believe my eyes, the case should not have gone to court never mind cost me my life. I was absolutely furious as the realisation came that the authorities had been at a blatant stitch up, they had made no mistake here this was a determined destruction of justice and some of the previous information that you have seen was only brought to my attention at this late point. Tracy Macalroy had given the police Nine different and conflicting statements (I had previously been made aware of five). Steven Madden and his friend and also IB and CB had all made a number of statements and with every contact with the police in the lead up to my arrest they had given more detailed and more damning statements that get more ridiculous as they go along. Anyone who looks at the statements of those five false witnesses can see that they were all terrorised by the police and they all subsequently committed perjury for the crown in order to facilitate my wrongful incarceration.

I tried desperately to get a new lawyer however the case was now a notorious fit up job with politicians behind it so no one had the balls to take it on. There are surprisingly few lawyers in Scotland who actually want to defend clients. Most work for the crown as double agents and are happy to sit down and cash the cheques with no fight. Life was extremely difficult for me, I cant even begin to describe the rage that was screaming out of my every pore. The paperwork for this case proves that it was an aggressive fit up and the perpetrators could not care less about my innocence or even about hiding their crimes. Such establishment crooks are never brought to account so why should they care? No decent human being would do that job in the first place so human decency is missing before they even begin.

The Big Issue and the Clydebank Post did me proud with plenty of positive stories, good on them for honest work and a refusal to be silent. Too many of the widespread media are muffled by manipulators. If you must read newspapers then you should stick to the smaller ones if you want to see the truth.

The trial judge report came in and it was so clear that Lord Emslie believed that I was innocent that a national newspaper did a front page story. Unfortunately they used a really ugly police mug-shot from this unlawful arrest. I'm not photogenic at the best of times but this one was truly horrific. They get all of their stories from the police and prosecutors and ministers so they cant risk upsetting them too much. They were helping me by mentioning my story but they also couldn't help themselves from siding with the authorities and they said that I was a career criminal. I have been jailed in the past for two silly fights and one robbery, if that makes me a career criminal then by that very reasoning you are a house builder if you fix up a shelf lay a carpet and paint your spare room.

They also said that Justin Macalroy had been killed by a hitman over a £50K drug debt. Yet he had plenty of money and one of his three cars alone was worth £90K so it is ridiculous to suggest that he could not pay £50K and had to die. Also most crucial is the fact that a neighbour heard Justin Macalroy having what she called a 'friendly conversation' on their dark street at 10pm which lasted a few minutes. She said that 'it went like the Jerry Springer show' with a blazing argument that was eventually broken by gunshots. That is not even remotely like a hitman murder. It was clearly a fight between two gangsters and she could hear both voices in the preceding conversation so the killer did not have a mask over his face at that point. So if the SDEA were there then they have photographs or film footage of the face of the actual killer and the crown have withheld that along with everything else. The SDEA reluctantly admitted that due to their four year surveillance of Justin Macalroy they knew for sure that I did not know him and had never met him and they admitted that I was not involved in drugs.

My people had a freedom campaign meeting in Temple primary school and I was lucky enough to phone while they were all there and when they heard that it was me on the phone they all cheered. I almost cried to hear such love after years of torture and hate. Some of them went on to put up 6000 protest posters in Glasgow, Perth, Dundee and Edinburgh. Paul McCluskey made a short film about my fight for justice and some of my people held a noisy protest outside Glasgow High Kangaroo court. Words cant express the respect and love I have for the good people who have fought for me. You all know who you are. Much love.

My personal battle was against my rage at the injustice, I battered the life out of the punch-bag and hammered into heavy weightlifting. It was the only way to stop myself from going over the fence and on a revenge rampage. They had blatantly screwed me over for life and I often had to physically roar and batter that punch-bag in my efforts to control my urges to punish those evil arrogant bastards. Even now I still have nuclear bombs exploding in my head and my heart when I think back to those dark days and think about the animals and what they have done to me. I have had years of practice now and am at last in almost complete control.

Jim Keegan spent the next TWO YEARS putting together an alleged powerful appeal case. The appeal court had been ready to hear my case months after the trial but Jim Keegan constantly asked for extensions and promised me that he was working so much and the case was so clearly a stitch up that I would be set free at the appeal court. I had no other lawyers and everyone else was trusting Jim Keegan so I forced myself to ignore my instincts and let him do the legal side while I continued my battle to stay calm enough to function and not go crazy on a revenge attack. It was taking all of my time and energy so it was easier to join everyone else and trust Jim Keegan to do his job.

You may wonder about my talk of revenge. As I often say, I'm not here to win any 'nicest guy in the world' competitions. I love people and I love peace however if someone tries to harm me or my loved ones then my instinct is to use violence for defence. In that sense you could say that I am not a very nice guy because I have used violence against bullies in the past. As I've grown up and recognised the nature of the justice system I only stop my natural urges because I am sick to death of the sight of police and prosecutors and judges and screws and jail and every other monstrous part of the system. My first instinct every time now is to ignore the provocation and walk away but they came and got me and the attack is twenty four seven for life. They did that in the full knowledge that I am innocent. My battle then for those next two years as I waited for an appeal hearing was internal, I've had to fight every single minute of every day and somehow try to convince myself that revenge violence is not the answer. It is the easiest way to get true justice and it would protect further innocent people from the monsters who targeted me however it is not the best way and it is not the right way.

Sam Poling and Dominic Gallagher of the BBC came up to see me in Shotts visit area and they quizzed me about every part of the case. Within a month they had made and aired a BBC Frontline Scotland programme about the injustice that I have suffered. They did not even touch on any of the crooked police and crown activities however the case against me is such an obvious nonsense that even the so called uncontroversial evidence has clearly been fabricated.

I had now suffered four long years of torture and Jim Keegan promised me that he did not even need the CCTV footage and I protested and asked him to keep trying to get the crown to obey the law and give us access to it. He promised me that he had the case beaten and what is even more sickening is that he promised my loved ones and absolutely guaranteed to get me set free at the appeal hearing.

The date eventually came up for the appeal and a large number of my supporters travelled through to Edinburgh to see me set free at last. Jim Keegan stood up and spoke nonsense for ten minutes, he did not lead ANY of my appeal points and only used a bullshit point about the jury and he even retracted that as he stood there in front of our eyes. Next the most notorious prosecutor in Scotland Alan Turnbull stood up and spoke non stop shit for five hours. He based his entire case on the evidence of Steven Madden observing a white car leaving the scene. Alan Turnbull did that in the full knowledge that the procurator fiscal in my case had been in possession of CCTV footage since before my arrest which proved that Steven Madden was not at the scene and neither was I or the white car. Alan Turnbull perverted the course of justice in order to keep an innocent man – me locked up for life. He also echoed the exact words of Tony Blair and said that the prosecution had brought forward a 'Powerful And Compelling Case'. They must all get the patter out of the same double speak dictionary. After Alan Turnbull's performance the (then) First minister of Scotland Jack McConnell rewarded him by putting him up for a top job as a High Court judge. He got the job and went on to instigate the outrageous perjury case against the innocent Sheridan family. Alan Turnbull has some cheek to do that to further innocents after he personally perverted the course of justice and lied to the appeal court judges during my case. Alan Turnbull is corrupt and is abusing his powerful position as a High Court judge. It is absolutely in the public interest to see him investigated and prosecuted for the crimes that he committed against me. He is a disgrace. His crooked character did not prevent him from becoming a High Court judge so that naturally leads us to wonder about the vetting process. What about the other 33 High Court judges, are they all as corrupt as Alan Turnbull?

My appeal hearing had been held back for two years by Jim Keegan and he had just blatantly thrown the fight in front of everyone. Whenever I had tried to speak to him during the bogus hearing his assistant had told me to be quiet or I would be thrown out of my own appeal! I had no clue what to do and sat there fuming in silence as I desperately hoped that he would get on to representing my interests and leading my evidence at some point but he never did. Suddenly it was all over and he had done nothing. That is what is so wrong with our kangaroo courts the accused and the victims are viewed as insignificant pieces on the black magic chessboard, it is all just a game to most lawyers and judges and all that they seem to care about is getting the statistics looking strong with convictions.

The appeal judges deferred the case and said that they would come back with a verdict at a later date. Instead of my promised walk to freedom I was taken back to the cells. A few people roared at Jim Keegan in the corridor and accused him of being an animal who had just blatantly helped the crown to destroy my appeal in front of everyone. After four years of torture and such high promises from Jim Keegan some of my people were crying and shouting outside the appeal court. Some hours later my dad had a heart attack. He survived thank goodness and is still with us. How much more can we take?

In my opinion you should only use Jim Keegan of Keegan Smith solicitors in Livingston if you want to help your prosecutors. I had reluctantly given him the benefit of the doubt after his abysmal performance at the trial however he blatantly screwed me over at the appeal and he was not shy about doing it. That is how debauched the Scottish legal system really is, fake defence lawyers the world over at least try to convince the defendants that they are working for them, but in Scotland they blatantly do you over irregardless of your innocence and they are not scared because there is no transparency or accountability and they are never ever brought to account. The police, prosecutors, fake defence lawyers and judges all like to pretend to themselves that they are part of a moral crusade and are only persecuting the guilty. Only a tiny amount of genuine defence lawyers stand against that deranged army.

It took a few agonising days for my dad to recover from his heart attack and my persecutors had never come so close to Armageddon. As soon as I was assured that my dad was back on his feet I went straight back to war in their legal arena. I sacked Jim Keegan then wrote a letter to each of the appeal judges who had been on the bench during my bogus hearing. I told them that they had no right to reach any verdict because they had not heard my appeal. I explained that Jim Keegan was at it and had helped the crown to keep my case buried. He had promised the world and when it got to court he had wilfully withheld my appeal points in order to help the crown. He had then sat there and let the prosecutor Alan Turnbull tell blatant lies and manipulate the bench. Alan Turnbull was blatantly perverting the course of justice and Jim Keegan sat in silence for him. The judges left me roasting for a further Three Months.

By the time I went back to court I still did not have a new lawyer. I stood alone and the Lord Justice General (the boss of the high court) Lord Cullen asked me about the letter. I stood up and repeated that Jim Keegan is a crook and had helped the crown by burying my appeal points denying me a fair hearing. Lord Cullen agreed and asked me if I could get a new solicitor and come back next week. I said yes and the new prosecutor John Beckett sat red faced in silence.

The prosecutor from the appeal Alan Turnbull as I said had been put up for a top job by Jack McConnell. So he had sent the next best in line for my outrageous injustice case, John Beckett. He is also a member of the Labour party, just a coincidence I'm sure. I managed to get the best defender in Scotland, the human rights solicitor Aamer Anwar to take my case and he brought in the best appeal QC in Scotland Margaret Scott. They both have formidable reputations and for the first time in years I was now actually represented by a legitimate defence team.

One week later we were back in the appeal court and unfortunately Lord Cullen had retired that week. The (then) First minister of Scotland Jack McConnell had put up for the top job Lord Hamilton. The three judges tried to set a few trap doors for Margaret Scott QC as she represented me but she was indestructible. She went on to explain that she had only spent one week so far looking at my case and already she could see clearly at least half a dozen points of appeal that Jim Keegan had inexplicably failed to raise. They tried to blame me for hiring him! They corrupt him and then blame me. Margaret Scott was having none of it and explained that it was not my fault and that I had been desperately trying to raise some of those points since before my trial. They eventually agreed with sanity and granted me the chance to have a legitimate appeal hearing where I would actually be represented by a defence team.

Over the next three weeks both Aamer Anwar and Margaret Scott did a mountain of work on the case and we went back to court for an informal procedural hearing. On the bench was Lord Osborne the one who had sentenced me to seven years for robbing that jewellers back in 1996. We don't have a legitimate appeal court in Scotland our High Court judges sit through trials one day while many naughty practices go on and the next day they sit on the appeal bench pretending to be interested in ending naughty practices and restoring justice. It is all a fraud and a waste of taxpayers millions, they should just shut the appeal court and openly tell victims of injustice to get fucked rather than go through years of pretence. We were only back in this court for a supposed procedural hearing when suddenly Lord Osborne and the others attacked Margaret Scott and started rambling on about the 'unusual circumstances'. The only thing that was unusual was that I refused to lay down in the face of injustice and had demanded my rights and managed to find a proper defence team. The crown were blaming me for crimes that they had committed against me. At one point Lord Osborne said "why don't we just throw this to the commission." Margaret Scott tried to protest at this outrageous statement and he cut her off. "He has had an appeal hearing and that appeal is refused."

They said it with less emotion than the judges on the talent shows on tv. Yet by refusing to even listen to my appeal points they had just sentenced me all over again to the absolute torture of wrongful imprisonment for life. They stood up to walk out and I jumped up and shouted, "this is a travesty, you couldn't spell justice."

The prosecutor John Beckett sat there with a fake tough guy scowl on his face. What a roaster. The (then) First Minister of Scotland Jack McConnell was apparently pleased with the extension of the injustice because he promoted John Beckett up to a top job as Solicitor General.

As for Colin Boyd the corrupt Lord Advocate who had brought the case against me, Jack McConnell made him a lifetime Peer. He is now Lord Boyd.

I had now been wrongfully arrested, had planted evidence and false witnesses put up against me, I had been denied my legal rights to the CCTV footage, I had been kept locked up illegally for two years before my trial, I had then been denied a fair trial in the face of crown agents perverting the course of justice, I had been kept locked up illegally for a further two years then denied a proper appeal hearing by my bogus defence lawyer Jim Keegan wilfully failing to raise any of my points of appeal and by the prosecutor Alan Turnbull perverting the course by telling lies to the bench. Then when I complained and actually managed to find legitimate legal representatives the crown had used a procedural hearing to go against the interests of justice and denied me the chance to have my points of appeal heard.

Most startling of all is the fact that they have never once even tried to pretend to be legitimate. Anyone can look at my case and see that it is a complete stitch up at every level. The police, prosecutors and judges are all allegedly working in the public interest yet they have all broken the law and denied me my rights in order to lock me up for life for a crime that I did not commit. Not one of them has obeyed the law or protected the public and they all deserve to be brought to account. Only a public inquiry could deliver that.

I was taken back to Shotts prison and again mere words could not describe my rage at the sickening catalogue of injustices that I had suffered. Before you can take your case to the European Court of Human Rights you have to exhaust all domestic avenues. That meant that I had to go where Lord Osborne had suggested and 'be thrown to the commission'.

The Scottish criminal cases review commission was set up in 1999 as a body allegedly independent of the courts whose remit is to investigate suspected miscarriages of justice. They have the power to seize any and all evidence and to force the court of appeal to permit victims of injustice to have a proper hearing. They are paid £1.3 Million per year in taxpayers money. They make many claims to be diligent impartial and independent and promise that they will review every case properly. However the statistics don't quite reflect those claims.

The SCCRC have so far looked at 887 cases where a suspected miscarriage of justice may have occurred. After their investigations they popped 820 of those cases in the bin and only sent 67 to the appeal court and the majority of them were bogus sentences and one was in fact a £25 fine! No harm to that person but our jails are bursting with injustice victims who are locked up for decades and clearing little cases like the small fine are suspiciously like massaging the statistics rather than trying to restore justice. As for the claim about being impartial if you look at their members you may question that one.

1) Chairman. The Very Reverend Graham Forbes CBE Provost of St Mary's Cathedral Edinburgh.
2) Sir Gerard Gordon QC CBE.
3) Sheriff Ruth Anderson QC.
4) Peter Duff Professor of criminal justice at Aberdeen University.
5) David Belfall, a retired civil servant.
6) James McKay, retired Deputy Chief Constable of Tayside police.
7) Gordon Bell QC.
8) Robert Anthony QC.
9) Professor Brain Caddy.
10) Chief Executive. Sheriff Gerard Sinclair.
11) Case worker, Stephen Lynn.
12) Case worker, Gordon Newall.

Not quite an independent body. They say that they will review all cases within nine months of an application yet they have so far taken more than Two Years on my case and they actually tortured me for the last eight months of that with continued false promises about the case being ready. I have suffered the most blatant injustice that Scotland has seen yet the SCCRC have stolen two years of my life and have not looked into even one point. All that they have done is steal £2.6 Million of taxpayers money over that period and have kept my case buried from the public and from justice.

After that two years of further torture they waited until New Years Eve and got a screw to hand me a 104 page report which served as an interim answer saying that they don't want to send my case back to the appeal court! The screw actually said "happy new year" before he handed me the pile of ridiculous lies from the SCCRC.

The human rights solicitor Aamer Anwar has worked tirelessly despite the crooked legal aid board denying me any funding. Paddy Hill and John McManus and Cathy at MOJO have also worked very hard alongside a freelance journalist Mark

Howarth. My local MSP Alex Neil and his friend the former police commander Ian McKie have also taken an interest and have put a lot of effort into investigating my case.

All of those wonderful human beings are desperately trying to represent justice and the public interest and have all submitted reports and letters to the SCCRC asking them to obey the law, do their job, look into my case professionally and impartially and to refer it back to the court of appeal where I can be represented by a legitimate legal team and can at last try to prove my innocence and get justice. If the SCCRC continue to assist the corrupt by covering up the crimes that have been and are being committed against me then they too should be brought into a public inquiry in order to answer (under oath) to their criminal actions. Who is pulling their strings? Who are they trying to protect? Some of the SCCRC commissioners are presiding over cases in their capacity as Sheriffs where they take the place of jurors and decide on innocence or guilt. Their actions in my case so far should bar them from such an important job. And again we must wonder about the vetting process and ask whether every Sheriff in Scotland is corrupt. To date they have shown that they could not care less about justice and are only interested in cover up. Ultimately everyone who has a dirty hand in this case have assisted the real killer of Justin Macalroy. That murderer has remained free for the past six years thanks to crooks in our legal system.

So here I sit. I have managed to endure six years of brutal torture and still stay strong and reasonably calm. My natural urges have tested me greatly, thankfully I have managed to stay sane and have not lost control to them. Where next? If the beasts got their way then I would remain locked up forever. They have an iron rule for innocent prisoners which they refer to as 'in denial of murder'. Even in a case like mine where they are physically in possession of evidence which proves my innocence they stick to the perverted I.D.O.M. rule. If an innocent prisoner refuses to tell lies and vindicate his persecutors by claiming to be guilty then they never grant parole.

Nothing and no one could ever put me on my knees, I would never tell lies and admit to a crime that even they know I did not commit therefore they will never set me free unless I get a legitimate appeal hearing. All four of my grandparents lived into their seventies and eighties. If I remain in jail then I wont last that long, I am suffering extreme torture and stress every single minute of every day (yes you do even have nightmares about the nightmare when you are sleeping). As each day passes the injustice gets extended by twenty-four hours and so the anger and stress rise along with it. Also ninety-six percent of prisoners smoke so the entire place is full of cancerous poison and the SPS refuse to provide smoke free wings. What is worse is that the American trend for super halls with hundreds of prisoners all packed in often two to a cell are proposed for the entire prison estate so if the cancer doesn't get you then the stress will. The regime in Shotts at the moment is manageable however overall the system still destroys people. Jail shortens life expectancy.

Here I am in this brutal system serving someone else's time. A legal team and my MSP are fighting ferociously for me and this is now a chance for my persecutors to finally behave themselves and obey the law by delivering justice.

As for the future I will never give in, it is my nature to fight in self defence anyone and anything for as long as it takes for me to win. To date they have managed to keep the fight for justice inside their kangaroo court arenas. We are at the point now where they will either allow me access to the illegally hidden evidence and grant me a fair hearing or they will use the SCCRC to close that last door.

I have been very patient over a painfully long period of time and have given them fair warning and every possible chance to obey the law. If they are so far gone with wickedness that they don't give me justice then I will begin round two and this time it wont be in their courts with everything stacked in their crooked interests. The arena will be elsewhere.

Before I go I must speak directly to some people. To the legitimate witnesses you did your public duty and told the truth so I thank you. To the perjurers, Tracy Macalroy you at least had an excuse for your crime, you were manipulated and brainwashed and I forgive you completely despite the damage you have done to me. Steven Madden and your friend I ask you both to come forward and tell the truth. What did the police do to you in order to persuade you to tell the catalogue of lies that cost me my life? Whatever it was I realise that you had little choice and are not the actual guilty party, I am convinced that it was the police so I also forgive you completely however I ask you to cleanse yourselves by coming forward and telling the truth. IB unfortunately you have now lost your 32 year old son. He was cut down by a sword in the street just as surely as I was cut down by the sword of injustice in court. You have now felt the pain that you caused my Dad when you told lies against me that resulted in me being wrongfully snatched away so I wonder if you will now do the right thing and come forward and tell the truth.

Jack McConnell MSP and Frank Roy MP I am convinced that you are crooks and that you took a bung of heroin money to persuade the police to make an arrest of a patsy for the murder of Justin Macalroy. If that is not true then prove it by doing a libel case and give your evidence and answer questions under oath.

Colin Boyd, Alan Turnbull, Alan McKay and John Beckett (to a lesser degree Beckett) you all wilfully and maliciously perverted the course of justice in order to jail for life an innocent man – me. When you who are there to administer the law become the ones who break it you are lost. Everything that you ever claimed to be has become a lie. I cannot think of a worse fate for anyone than being born as one of you who have evil souls. Your descendants will feel your shame for eternity.

As for you police, in particular DCI Gordon McConnell, DS John Ferguson, DC Ian Thompson, ex-DC Colin Morgan and you woman hater DC Alan Rae I have tried to convince myself that you all believed somehow that you were fitting up a guilty man but when I look at your actions especially you Gordon McConnell and you John Ferguson I can see that you are all snakes who commit heinous crimes simply because you can. You all appear to have a rapist mentality destroying people for your own perverted pleasure. And terrorising women is clearly your nature. What disgusting creatures you are.

All of you civil servants who fit up and lock up for life innocent people should yourselves be jailed forever. The legal system is completely corrupt of course and will protect you from any prosecution but times change, things happen, justice can suddenly prevail. Despite the lamentable history of our courts it would be wise if you prepare yourselves for the unexpected.

Keep your eyes open and you may get to see true justice.

To the reader, I can only apologise for ending this book here before the final result of my battle for justice. I have a website,

www.whygage.com

on there you can watch short films or read the latest news section if you want to learn of any future developments. Victory will be mine one day because I refuse to lose. With a positive mindset, a strong will and enough courage you can do like the Angel said and turn any situation into a Win-Win.

I have suffered a great deal but I am not chasing sympathy. I do believe that fate acts upon each of us for a purpose and with that in mind I always turn every situation to my advantage no matter how gruesome it may be I try my best to use it for good.

My wee Gran used to say that god will never give you a burden that is too heavy for your shoulders to carry. Although this burden is the weight of an anvil round my neck I am strong enough to carry it and as you have seen I am trying to use it to help others with knowledge.

I believe that if you can help even one person then the pain and effort are worth it. I pray that at least one soul (perhaps a thirteen year old version of someone like me) will get a copy of this book and will be enlightened and inspired to pursue a more positive path in life.

The next chapter is a bit extraneous to my personal story but it is relevant to everyone in the U.K. and should serve as an aid for anyone who is searching for truth. Please read it with my compliments.

Justice for all. Peace and Love. In the name of Scotland.

Bonus chapter

jus gladii

I believe that I have seen our true history and even today the evidence mounts up. What were the MP Frank Roy, the MSP Jack McConnell, the (then) Home Secretary John Reid and MI5 agents and senior police all doing socialising with suspected heroin barons who had been under SDEA surveillance for four years? Why were those suspects Justin Macalroy and his dad Tommy Macalroy not arrested after their friends (who they left in Estonia) were caught trying to smuggle millions of pounds worth of heroin into Scotland? Why was one of those friends later claiming that they were all MI5 licensed heroin barons who only got caught because the Estonian police made a move? Why have hundreds of suspected heroin barons been permitted to openly thrive for decades without ever being arrested? If MI5 are not behind the heroin trade in Britain then why have dozens of them been shuttling over to Afghanistan since November 2001?   Consider the following once again. There are tens of thousands of drug related arrests every year in the U.K. There are roughly ninety thousand prisoners in British jails and more than ninety percent are either drug addicts or low level dealers. Thousands of large shipments have been seized yet there is never a full dry up of drugs.

In the 1960's when civil rights organisations began protesting worldwide there was a sudden MI5 effort to stir up massively the Irish troubles. And worldwide there was also a sudden new wave of illegal drugs spreading everywhere creating fractured communities and societies resulting in weakened peoples.

There is evidence that the CIA and MI5 personally funded the Afghani drug lords. In 1979 Russia tried to cut off the bulk of the finances to the British and American security services, they did that by invading Afghanistan to go after the heroin. Afghanistan was then as it is now the supplier of eighty percent of the worlds illegal heroin stock. The CIA and MI5 immediately made contact with maniac radicals – the Taliban. They funded armed and trained the Taliban into a ferocious fighting force and with USA and UK coalition weapons they eventually beat the Russians back out of their country.

The heroin supply was guaranteed again so the 'good guys' of the CIA and MI5 simply pulled out and left the maniacs armed to the teeth with literally millions of pounds worth of weaponry. The Taliban then set about radicalising as many people as possible into their own twisted way of thinking and in particular they used their new power to persecute women.

It took twenty years before they turned their attention to the west. And just like the Russians had intended to do, the Taliban went after the heroin in order to bankrupt the CIA and MI5. If they had been left alone then ninety percent of crime in America and Britain would be erased and so the criminal justice army would be obsolete. There would no longer be that excuse to seize legal and human rights and the masses would no longer be suffering the terror of the junkie crime waves. With their minds cleared of those fears the people would now have the capacity to wake up and possibly even recognise their true enemies. The characters who rule both countries were not about to let such positive things happen to the people.

In 1999 the poppy crop in Afghanistan was at an all time high, the drug lords had made their country the worlds number one heroin producer and by 2000 they had a bumper crop of a massive 4000 tons of raw opium. It was at that point when the Taliban decided to attack the American CIA, the British MI5 and the Pakistani SIS by suddenly jailing all of the Afghani drug lords and they passed a sentence of death onto anyone caught making heroin. By 2001 they had almost eradicated opium production altogether and satellite pictures showed that the crop was down from 4000 tons to just 134 tons. The Taliban tactic was going splendidly, every country was jostling to buy the crops from Burma and South America and there was simply not enough to go round.

On the 9th of September 2001 after nine months of struggling to get more heroin two planes were flown into the twin towers in New York. Again please read the work and watch the films on Alexjones.com to widen your perspective. America and Britain immediately blamed Saudi radicals and their leader Osama bin Laden however they did not pick a fight with their Saudi pals, instead they accused the Taliban in Afghanistan of harbouring Osama bin Laden and his gang.

The USA and UK ordered the Taliban to hand over the fugitives or face the consequences and within eight weeks they declared war on the Taliban and bombed the life out of Afghanistan before invading. They have been in there now for more than six years and cant find Osama bin Laden to hand him over to themselves. Even with a $25 Million bounty on his head they cant find him therefore it is reasonable to believe that before the invasion neither could the Taliban so they are not guilty of that charge and that means the war is illegal.

Now consider this. Ninety percent of crime in America and Britain is heroin related. In November 2001 they invaded and seized control of Afghanistan, the producer of eighty percent of the worlds heroin. Did the Americans and British take the opportunity to eradicate overnight the nightmare crime waves in their countries? They could easily have sprayed the crops and destroyed completely the 134 tons worth that the Taliban had not yet got round to eradicating. Did they pay the farmers a few quid compensation and spray the crops? No. They set free every drug lord who had been jailed by the Taliban. Next they gave the entire country to the biggest drug lord and told him to put up a front man as president – he rubbed his hands with glee and eagerly made his own brother the new president of Afghanistan. Next in a similar scam that they use back home they gave the drug barons hundreds of thousands of pounds of taxpayers money as bogus payment for 'security' on the army camps! They invade the country and take over then spring drug gangsters from jail and hand it all to them and pay fortunes of our money for the drugs under the guise of 'security'. You couldn't make this up.

What about the crops did they destroy them? Here are the figures since the USA and the UK took control of Afghanistan. Remember the rag tag gang of Taliban got the crops down from 4000 tons to 134 tons in just one year and we could have then sprayed the crops and eradicated the lot in one day. How well did the USA and the UK really do? (2001 _ 134 tons. Taliban eradication.) 2002 _ 1400 tons. 2003 _ 3500 tons. 2004 _ 4500 tons. 2005 _ 5000 tons. 2006 _ 6100 tons. And in 2007 it was up to a sickening 8200 tons. Do you see a pattern that should not be there? Who gains from this? Not OBL or the Taliban.

Please take into consideration the fact that legitimate

medicinal requirements for the entire world are met by only 680 tons each year. Apparently the CIA and MI5 could buy that from their pals in South America when they are down buying their Cocaine. Why did they not spray the poppy crops in Afghanistan and why have they been battering into a serious effort to ramp up massively the production of the drug that causes ninety percent of the crime in the very countries that they are allegedly out to protect?

They need the heroin in order to keep the people crushed under the junkie crime waves that raise an estimated £8 billion per year in the UK alone. And they need that crime epidemic in order to justify their own £15 Billion per year budget and the police army, and the Four Point Five Million cctv cameras on our streets, and the mass employment of their robot pals that comes from the vast prison population, and the relentless attack on our legal and human rights.

Bolstered by their successful illegal war in Afghanistan they set their sights higher and just seventeen months after that invasion they told lies again and this time invaded Iraq, one of the most oil rich countries on the planet. One million innocent Iraqi's now lay murdered, four million are refugees and one Billion Muslims worldwide are now at greater risk of being targeted for brainwashing by maniac radicals who want to ignore the blessed teachings of Mohamed and focus solely on the evil words sneaked into the religious books by the tyrant rulers of old and do useless terrorist attacks on innocent people.

The Nazi's dropped literally hundreds of thousands of bombs on Britain and still the people never gave up so even if the radicals could persuade that many morons to blow themselves up it would still get them nowhere. They could (as MI5 have suggested) target our nuclear power stations but they would only be inviting our nuclear bombs onto their heads in every Muslim country on earth, who wins there? Even if they could kill Bush or Bliar or Brown or even the royals there are millions of similar evil souls who would immediately take their place and revenge would be swift and devastating.

In my opinion the greatest threat to Muslims today is the people who are preaching hate and violence. I urge you potential terrorists to ignore the lies and study every war that the British rulers have fought, you will learn that you cant beat such ferocious enemies with violence. Look to the only man who ever beat the berserk mob – Gandhi. If you are so angry that you want to blow shit up then you should first take the time to study him and if you have any brains or courage then you will recognise and accept how futile violence against crazies really is. Don't behave like scared little monkeys, use your brains. You should never kill anyone however if you must lose your temper then first take a good look at the people who are trying to preach hate. They are the true enemies of Islam. There are more than one Billion Muslims in the world, do you not find it a bit strange that the cleric who radicalised the guys (who went on to commit the 7/7 bombings in London) was an American. I could be wrong of course but there is no question in my mind that he was a CIA operative. Who benefits from the terror? It is not any help to Muslims. It only serves to help the people who run America and also those who run Britain and want to create a prison planet with no legal and no human rights for the ordinary citizens. So my little would be terrorist friends it is in your interests to put down the bombs and pick up the books. Peace non-violence and profit-hurting civil disobedience are the only ways to defeat tyrants.

As for the good people of Britain you are perceived as a threat and treated as such because your rulers are gangsters who have seized your property through theft by inheritance and are using manufactured crime and the law and the courts as weapons of war against you. What can you do?

Look at them. Tony Blair declared that all tobacco advertising would be banned at sporting events. Tony Blair was then invited to dinner by a motor racing mogul who promptly gave him a £1 Million donation. He came back with that money tucked into his Labour pocket and declared that tobacco advertising was still banned – except at motor racing. That very day Blair's wife Cherie Booth was doing her job as a court prosecutor (she is now a judge surprise-surprise) and she asked the judge to jail an old man who had not paid his council tax. He was not a conscientious abstainer he was genuinely skint yet she was trying to get him sent to jail on the very day that her husband was taking a bung to allow advertising of a drug that kills the addicts and those around them. What makes it worse is that Tony Blair's number two in the Labour party John (two jags) Prescott had failed to pay £11,000 on his three homes! Cherie was not shouting to get him locked up in jail and still you voted for them.

They use heroin to cause ninety percent of crime in Britain and they never jail their heroin baron police informers and still you vote for them. They invaded Afghanistan on a lie and ramped up massively the heroin production and still you vote for them. They tell more lies and invade Iraq and go on to murder one million innocent people and create four million desperate refugees and still you vote for them. One million of you march onto the streets in protest screaming for justice and peace and they completely ignore you and still you believe that the royals and their sick advisors are not running the country and that your chosen representatives are and that you have a say in it.

Tony Blair's brother is a High Court Judge and he recently knocked back two innocent people from the appeal court with a ridiculous excuse about false witnesses having no reason to tell lies! The front man Tony Blair steps aside, Gordon Brown who was knee deep in every atrocity signing the cheques on the illegal wars and the mass imprisonment of British citizens now jumped forward and took the job as the new pretend leader and still you vote for them.

Our true rulers have proven themselves to be warmongers and gangsters, illegal wars, genocide, worldwide drug dealing, mass imprisonment and absolute control of innocent people are not crimes in their warped minds. Being poor and unable to pay your bills is considered an extremely serious crime and you will be sent to jail for that.

They all openly socialise with their heroin barons because they are above the law, there is no transparency or accountability as long as the crimes are for the Crown. The Conservatives did exactly the same things with their heroin barons. Their former Home Secretary Michael Howard even went so far as openly getting a Royal pardon for two of his heroin baron pals who had been sentenced to twenty years each in Liverpool. I cant remember exactly if they were his friends or his cousins friends, essentially he contacted the Queen and told her that a mistake had been made and two men had been sentenced to twenty years each when they should never have been arrested due to their status as informers. She immediately pardoned them and they were set free. The message again being that you can commit any crime even importation and distribution of massive amounts of heroin as long as it is done for the man and you grass on patsy's to keep the public blind.

It doesn't matter which one of the three coalition parties you vote into 'power' they are all serfs for the monarchy, that is why your wishes and needs are the very last things on their list and are only ever mentioned in the run up to elections.

In a famous speech Caesar once said that when you beat the drums of war the people panic and if you can stoke that into terror then they will beg you to take away their rights if that is what you pretend to require in order to protect them.

Hitler used that same idea when he bombed his own parliament and blamed the communists (the terrorists of the day back then). He used that 'terrorist attack' as an excuse to suspend all legal rights. Most of you know what happened next and if you don't then please look it up.

The British rulers just like Hitler have adopted the tactics of Caesar and used the Irish troubles as an excuse to turn Britain and London in particular into a prison. Next came the Taliban (who the UK had funded and trained).

One attack in London on 7/7 has been blamed on such radicals. Every single one of the victims of that atrocity deserves our respect and blessings and no one could ever speak ill of them of course but we must put things into perspective. There were less than 100 direct victims of the 7/7 attack. Between 1969 and 1999 there were One Thousand deaths in police cells in the U.K. That figure shows you that the police could have possibly murdered ten times more people in Britain than the so called Muslim terrorists. It's not 'just' criminals who are locked up in police cells, it can happen to anyone.

Add to the figure of one thousand deaths the incalculable amount of innocent members of the public who have lost their freedom for life at the hands of British police and the total statistics now show you that our police are proven to be literally hundreds of times more of a deadly threat to us than foreign terrorists could ever be. Yet our rulers don't investigate the police or curb their powers in fact they have used the attacks on 7/7 as an excuse to go to war against the people and they are seizing more and more legal and human rights and are giving the police More powers over the innocent people. They took that attack on 7/7 and they used the media to bomb you over and over again until you believe that you are at war and in some sort of danger from foreign terrorists, but it is the psychopaths in Buckingham palace and Westminster who have you in their sights not foreign radicals.

Our rulers have us hoodwinked, brainwashed and terrorised. They have spent the past forty years seizing our rights and turning Britain into a prison. They have recently proposed to forcibly take the fingerprints of everyone who gets on a plane. Please look at what they did to Shirley McKie and David Asbury when they got their fingerprints. They are sneakily taking children's prints under the guise of library passes and taking their DNA under the guise of drug tests and alcohol breath tests. Please look at what they did to me when they got my DNA. There was a recent proposal to take a DNA sample from every serving police officer because they are contaminating crime scenes and some defendants are taking advantage of the unknown DNA profiles. The police refused to comply and openly admitted that they did not trust their colleagues and believed that it would be too much of a risk of being stitched up by having the DNA subsequently planted. All new police have to give a sample but the 16,000 Scottish police are determined to stay safe and not let anyone get a sample of their DNA. They well know that it is very simple and easy to take that sample and grow it then plant it at a crime scene or on any object from a crime scene. If you are wise then you will fight to the death to prevent the gangsters from getting your fingerprints or DNA or those of your children. Boycott the airports and airlines who try it for starters.

In ten years time what will the government have done? What will they be doing? Nothing nice that's for sure. After buttering us up for the past seven years with the terrorist scare stories they have now got the media to change the bogey man. Violence has not significantly risen on our streets but the media have been ordered to report as many violent crimes as possible especially if it involves kids. That blanket reporting creates the impression of a sudden crime wave and the public think that we have chaos and people are now terrified that their loved ones (predominately the teenagers) will be killed or will even kill and the resulting fear and paranoia fragments society. Everyone on the street is now being viewed as a potential knife wielding killer who should be locked up for a zillion years. After another few months of this propaganda reporting, the government will call for emergency legislation to solve the problem – more legal and human rights will be destroyed and the manipulated masses are so blind with fear that they will sigh with relief.

The lack of knowledge about the true route of violence makes the people blindly panic and want to lash out with demands for more severe prison sentences. In America they have the most severe prison terms on earth and the result is the worst offenders and crime rates because jail is not a cure it is a punishment that comes along after the crime and it damages the prisoners and makes them even worse. In Scandinavia they have the most lenient prison sentences and the result is the lowest crime rates because they don't torture the offenders they target the offending behaviour with fair treatment and attempts at rehabilitation.

Even jail sentences of one million years each for carrying a knife would only change the weapon not the criminal. You have to educate the kids early because once they are carrying a weapon it is too late. That is why the government only ever get you to focus on this useless late stage and scream for heavier sentences. They need the violence to continue because severe punishments and less legal rights for one crime gets quickly turned into severe sentences for all crimes and less legal rights for everyone.

Please understand that out of a population of 60 million souls there are only a tiny minority of people in Britain who break the law. The route causes are completely ignored and the blind panic bogus solutions are intended to make the criminals far worse with brutal jails and disproportionate sentences because our politicians are corrupt and just like taking a £1 Million bung for advertising poisonous tobacco they take orders from big business. The true targets of all of these anti crime right wing Draconian attacks is the innocent workers of Britain. Less rights for one group (criminals) leads to less rights for all (workers) and the fewer rights that workers have, the greater the profits for the bosses who give the orders to the puppet politicians.

You are being lied to and manipulated by maniacs and when they get the media to scare you and drive you into a panic you are easy to beat to the point where they can even scream that they want to protect you by taking away Your rights and even by locking up in brutal jails ten thousand teenage children and many of you will agree and actually want it to happen.

Poor people who cant pay the bills go to jail while rich politicians who wont pay the bills go free. Otherwise decent people who defend themselves with violence go to jail while the entire government sign up to illegal wars for queen and country and murder one million innocent people and they remain free. Can you see what sort of population will be left alive after a century or two of such madness?

If Osama bin Laden and his followers managed to kill our rulers and took over then came on tv and tried to tell you that they were going to seize your legal and human rights, would lock you up without charge for 42 days and would put you on trial with false witnesses against you who had their identities hidden and actual serving police officers who swear allegiance to the rulers would be openly allowed to sit on your jury where you are looking at life in jail, then there would be a revolution and rightly so. You would all be on the streets demanding the destruction of the maniac terrorists who wanted to smash every legal and human right that your ancestors have all fought and died for. You would hammer the palaces and parliaments into the ground. Yet when the terrorists have white skin and no beards and they wear a suit instead of a robe then you bend over and take it all! What is going on in people's heads? No wonder every psychiatrist in the country is ill, the people are impossible to understand and trying it would drive anyone crackers. Can you see the insanity that is screaming from our rulers? Besiege your MP and MSP and demand sanity and a reversal of the attack on your rights, demand freedom and justice and equality and assure them that they will not be getting any votes until they openly stop and reverse this destruction of freedom.

Once they have armed police killers and two cameras on every street (not just the main roads) and they have a satellite traced radio frequency indicator chip inside every passport and id card that you are all forced to carry and once they get rid of paper money and force you all to use credit cards and once they have invented just a few more criminal offences it will all be too late.

They have already created out of thin air Three Thousand new criminal offences in the past ten years alone, try yourself to invent just one and you will get an idea of how deranged these people really are. They jailed more people during that decade than in the past fifty years put together. Despite the enormous prison population, crime levels remain the same because most organised crime like drug importation and distribution is committed by licensed police informers who are very rarely ever arrested. After ten long years of destroying family units by jailing so many people the children of those prisoners have grown into teenagers and the social carnage that results from having tens of thousands of jail orphans is now spreading onto our streets.

The families have been ripped apart by the government mass imprisonment policies and that damaged the children. Rather than help those kids, the establishment now want to jail all of them too and have announced a massive prison building programme. The heart of Mother Nature herself must be breaking.

They put up millions of police cameras on the streets yet crime levels are not dented. Those cameras are not for crime prevention or detection they are for war. Just in case you all ever wake up to what is really going on they want to be able to see every inch of the battlefield. They never ask your permission they just batter the cameras up everywhere because they want to create apathy. They want you to believe that you are in danger and that you are a helpless victim who can only be saved by them. They are now adding to the cctv with unmanned military drone spy-planes flying over our streets using powerful lenses to watch you outdoors and thermal cameras to spy on you while you are at home. The excuse for this latest rape? Anti social behaviour. The truth is that you can protect yourself, you are not a helpless victim, again get organised and into community groups as large as possible and demand that your local MP and MSP protect you by locking up all sex offenders in asylums for life and give heroin out free on prescription and then your streets will be the safest in the world. Now you can demand the removal of the cameras and an end to all intrusive and unnecessary surveillance.

It will soon be in small print in some legal Bill that everything is illegal if they can pretend that the innocuous act could perhaps lead to a crime. Already looking at internet sites about terrorists can see you getting sentenced to long term imprisonment as a 'potential' terrorist. A young woman was recently jailed for writing poems about terrorists. The government are trying to make it illegal to write a book if you have any previous convictions (ever been done for speeding?) because tyrants do everything in their power to keep the truth from the people. Hitler burned books and killed writers, Stalin persecuted writers during his entire time in power. If the law proposed by the London government against people with a previous conviction writing a book had been in place sooner then the world would have lost a great many literary masterpieces. They will eventually ban all foreign travel for people with a previous conviction and for anyone else who is a suspect – that is you.

Already they are trying to introduce a brutal law which will allow them to hide the identity of witnesses in trials to protect them from the accused but the state is millions of times more of a threat to each defendant than he could ever be to any witness so that is not a balance. Next the jury judge police prosecutor and even the defence lawyer will be protected from the defendants, secret trials will be here and no one will have a chance.

In 2004 after ten years of the drug tests in jails were such a success in creating a crushed prison population suffering under a manufactured heroin plague the Labour party introduced those drug tests into two Schools in England. They dickied up the exam results after one year and pretended that more kids were passing exams due to now being drug free. They will soon make drug tests mandatory in every state run school (to tackle drugs, knife crime, violence, potential terrorism etc). Once they put blanket cctv cameras (with mikes) in every school 'to protect the kids' they could replace the teachers with secret police interrogators who could use the children as an aid to spy on the parents and also to asses which of the pupils are brighter than the rest and so are potential anti authority figures. The brightest ones could be forcibly employed by the state and if they refuse or do not conform then later they could be jailed. Your children.

Even as these things are happening you continue wasting your time watching football or the soaps on tv or celebrity stories while the people in power smash every legal and human right and try to spy on your every move, word and thought . It is important to do the things that you enjoy of course but you are partying at the back of the Titanic and if you just pay some attention to reality you can use your vote to shout at the Captain and force him to change direction and avoid the iceberg. You can use the bogus democracy against them by actually voting And making demands to get a legitimate democratic system with proper representation for the people not the corporations if you just pay attention, learn the truth then form community groups and fight for your rights.

If you fail to do that then in my opinion the best possible thing that you can do for yourself and more importantly for your descendants is escape off this island before it gets completely locked down. You don't have very long my friends, it is time for action.

If it is not your nature to run then your only option is to struggle I will not pretend to know the best method of struggle that you should use but I do genuinely believe that you must do something. If you live in England then you will need a wiser teacher than me because I can see no solution for you. In Scotland I personally believe that we may have a chance if we get independence but that seems like an impossible achievement given voter apathy and natural fear of change. I don't know much about the politics of the SNP but I have looked at the money situation.

Experts are certain that there is enough oil under the North sea to make Scotland one of the richest countries in Europe by a long way. The oil money has been stolen from us for the past thirty years. People in the media are ordered by the oil thieves to say that there is not enough money for Scotland to be independent but remember that the media once screamed that the NHS was a terrible idea and would bankrupt Britain, where would we be if the people listened to that shower? The truth is that Thirty Billion Barrels of oil remain under our sea and at an average price of $120 per barrel (£60 at the average exchange rate) that is far more money than Scotland would need to survive. Financially it could be done so perhaps we should all be bold, remember our true history and vote to be a free and independent republic and take care of ourselves for once.

The only sensible alternative is to get off this island while you still have the chance. You don't need to be a psychic or a genius to see what is coming and where this country is heading.

We are ruled by tyrants who have been using terrorist attacks and manufactured crime trends to terrify and keep us occupied while they destroy our human rights and put in place every piece on their Black Magic chessboard. The biggest threat to them is you the good people. You are their enemy and their targets not a few hundred gangsters, most of whom are MI5 licensed grasses anyway. And not a few hundred terrorists, most of whom are fear driven brain damage victims who want to behead a guy for drawing a cartoon. Both of those groups are tiny in number and would be very easy to stop overnight. The true rulers wont stop them because they need them as an excuse so that by the time you realise it is you who are the actual targets it will be too late they will already have you beaten in Checkmate.

They are so greedy that their ultimate dream is a sixty million strong slave labour population. That insane greed also makes them terrified of losing power or even losing you slaves so they want a prison country with absolute control maintained with seized human rights, complete surveillance of every word and action for every life, a murderous legal system, a massive prison population and terror attacks. With all of that they have the ingredients for absolute rule and maximum profits. That is the real future in Britain while these maniacs remain in power. It is their nature, it is everything that they have been working towards for many generations, and if you continue to do nothing then perhaps it is the inevitable outcome.

I have personally suffered extreme horrors at the hands of their lackeys and as a result I have often found it impossible to write without passion or to avoid using derogatory names or labels. Please believe me that my words were only ever intended to wake you up never to stir you up so you must not hate them no matter what you or I or anyone else thinks of them they are still human beings and should never be targeted or harmed in any way other than self defence. Hatred and violence are the cause of the problem not the cure.

In this book I have brought you many disturbing truths however I have not been trying to frighten you, I do not believe in unnecessary fear. Like the saying goes, a brave man dies only once – a coward dies every single time that he fears death.

Do not fear the tyrants, they can only continue if you remain asleep and closed off to reality. Wake up. Open your eyes, open your mind and open your heart. Don't be lazy. Think for yourself. Question. Analyse. Conclude and then take serious action whether it be your time to run away or your time to fight back, it is your time.

Coming soon

Curio by William Gage

Curio is book one of a crime fiction trilogy written by a man who has seen and done enough to enable him to take you on a roller-coaster ride through the Glasgow underworld.

It is the story of a vast criminal brotherhood so secretive that they have no name, so successful that they have survived in business since World War Two and so professional that they have been involved in literally thousands of lucrative jobs in a multitude of mayhem predominantly armed robberies all over Europe.

Curio takes you into the organisation alongside two young men who are head-hunted in and onto a life of professional crime. If you ever wondered how proper crooks manage to get rich, or about the ultimate adrenalin chasing, or the structures and activities of the true underworld then **Curio** is the book for you.

Curio is on sale soon, keep an eye on the website whygage. com or ebay.co.uk for further details.